COVER CREDITS

Publisher's Cataloging-in-Publication Data

provided by Five Rainbows Cataloging Services

Names: Walsh, C.T., author.

Title: Down with the dance / C.T. Walsh.

Description: Bohemia, NY : Farcical Press, 2019. | Series: Middle school mayhem, bk. 1. | Summary: Join Austin on his journey through the tumultuous waters of middle school. | Audience: Grades 5 & up. | Also available in ebook and audiobook formats.

Identifiers: ISBN 978-1-950826-01-8 (paperback)

Subjects: LCSH: Bildungsromans. | CYAC: Middle school students--Fiction. | Middle schools--Fiction. | Dance parties--Fiction. | Bullying--Fiction. | Friendship--Fiction. | Humorous stories. | BISAC: JUVENILE FICTION / Social Themes / Adolescence & Coming of Age. | JUVENILE FICTION / School & Education. | JUVENILE FICTION / Humorous Stories. | JUVENILE FICTION / Boys & Men.

Classification: LCC PZ7.1.W35 Do 2019 (print) | LCC PZ7.1.W35 (ebook) | DDC [Fic]--dc23.

For my Family

Thank you for all of your support

Middle school. I mean, am I right? You might think it's appropriately named because, well, it's smack dab in the middle of high school and elementary school (why isn't it called low school?), but to me it's more like muddle through school. And that's on good days. On bad days, it's medieval torture school. Everyone talked it up about how awesome it was with more freedom, new friends, and easy electives like napping and finger painting. But all I got was a Wednesday morning fart in the face (after Taco Tuesday), or in other words, a new principal who hated my guts.

Before we get into that, allow me to introduce myself. Austin Davenport here, and this is my story. Buckle up, it's going to be a bumpy ride. I'm just going to come right out and say it. No suspense. No mystery. There are two villains in this story, Principal Buthaire (he says it's French, but everyone calls him Butt Hair) and my brother, Derek. They are a match made in heaven, because my brother has the prized family butt chin, which means that everyone, including my parents, likes him more than me. At least it seems that way to me most of the time. Seriously, it's like he has a teeny tiny baby's butt on his chin. I don't know why everyone thinks it's so awesome. They've never seen the dark side of the butt chin. I don't even want to get into it, but let's just say that the cute little baby bottom ain't all that pretty when the dude eats chocolate pudding. I make myself feel better by calling him Butt Face, mainly behind his back, but sometimes I have the guts to whisper it when he's got his headphones on.

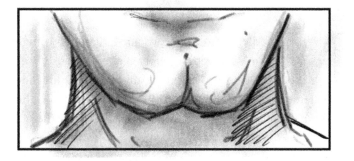

My parents are pretty smart people, but for some reason, they don't seem to realize that my brother is a putz. Never was it more apparent to me than during our first year of middle school together.

I should probably start at the beginning. I know it's confusing, the beginning of middle school, but try to keep up. It was the first day of sixth grade, our first year in Cherry Avenue Middle School. I know it sounds all sweet, warm, and fuzzy, but I assure you it was barely better than a flaming bag of poop. And when your brother is Derek Davenport, unfortunately, you get to know flaming bags of poop. I don't know where he gets it all.

Anyway, Cherry Avenue had a new principal because the old one was fired. Last year, the old principal let the eighth graders duct tape him to the wall for charity, which was fine and raised a lot of money for sick kids, but the students liked it so much that hordes of kids just started taping him to the walls every day. Pretty soon, the school was in chaos. My town implemented a new rule where you had to have ID or at least a mustache to buy more duct tape, but by that point, it was too late. Principal Puma had lost control and there was no turning back. So they brought in a former prison warden. I don't know that for certain, but I'd bet my brother's life on it that it's true.

So it was the morning of the first day of school. I was reasonably excited, but also nervous. I liked school, outside of the fact that I have to be there with other kids. I stood at the bus stop with my best friend, Ben Gordon, and my next-door neighbor and friend that's a girl (not girlfriend), Sammie Howell, talking coding. I know what you're thinking, no, we weren't the coolest kids, but coding's not just for the geeks anymore. Full disclosure, though. I'm pretty much a geek.

My brother, Derek, tossed a football leisurely with a few

of the older kids from our neighborhood. He was annoy-
ingly good at sports, well, almost everything, especially
tormenting me. He's eleven months older than me, and as it
so happens, was born in January, putting us in the same
grade. Lucky me. It's such a wonderful life experience
having your older, bigger, better-at-everything, butt-chinned
brother in school with you.

Stevie Stroudsburg overthrew the football. It tipped my
brother's fingers and helicoptered over toward us, stopping
at my feet. I gave it a quick tap over to my brother with the
hopes that he wouldn't get too close and say something to
embarrass or ridicule me.

"Thanks," he muttered. He turned back toward his
friends, and then back toward me. "Hey, you memorize your
locker combo yet? I hope I remember mine."

"Of course. 35-7-21," I said confidently, and without
thinking. I thought I caught a smirk surface on his annoying
face before he turned to continue his football catch.

"Oh, my God," I said to Ben and Sammie. "Do you think
he'll remember my combo?" I asked, beginning to sweat.

"He wouldn't do anything bad with it, even if he did,"
Sammie said. My brother could burn down the town and
turn himself in and she still wouldn't believe it. She's had a
crush on Derek for as long as I can remember. Hey, nobody's
perfect.

I looked at Ben for some assurance I could believe in. He
always gave it to me straight, even if he knew I wouldn't like
the answer. "Dude, you're in trouble. I'd ask Zorch for a new
lock as soon as you get to school."

"Who is Zorch?" Sammie asked, as the bus turned the
corner and headed our way.

"He's the custodian. You haven't heard of Zorch? He's a
janitorial legend," Ben answered.

"That's not a thing," Sammie said as she looked to me for support.

"He's kind of right. I hear he once caught three kids in a snare trap for trying to steal back something Zorch confiscated. They were dangling upside down in the hallway for the whole period before he let them down."

"That didn't happen." Sammie shook her head and frowned. "And I'm sure he'll love me anyway."

"Zorch doesn't make many friends. Just don't get on his bad side."

"Like asking for a new lock on the first day?" I questioned nervously.

"Yeah, like that," Ben responded, unhelpfully.

The bus rolled up and we all gathered in line, waiting for the doors to open.

"Here goes nothing," I muttered so only Ben could hear me.

"Just keep your head down and mouth shut. Grab the first seat you can find closest to the front," Ben said.

I nodded, but wasn't sure if I should risk ridicule by sitting back closer to my brother. I was still worried about the lock combination. I wanted to repeat fake numbers with the hopes that he would forget my real combo. I climbed onto the bus, forced a smile at the driver, and chickened out by diving into the third seat next to Ben. Sammie slid into the seat across the aisle with Vickie Olsen, a sometimes quiet, sometimes annoying girl from around the block.

The bus ride in went reasonably well. There were a few random spitballs, but all in all, pretty harmless. Ben and I made it to Advisory, which my parents called, Home Room, with little trouble. It's where we get advised to keep our mouths shut and listen to the morning announcements.

I sat next to Ben. We looked up at the speaker above the

door as it crackled, awaiting the announcements. I'm not sure why everyone looked at the speaker, but we all did. There was a tapping and then a whiny voice squeaked, "Good morning. This is Principal Buthaire." Most of the kids chuckled, already knowing his nickname. "Today, we enter a new era of education. Your Advisory teachers will be passing out the new rule books. Please read them and commit them to memory. They will be strictly enforced."

I looked over at Mrs. Callahan, as she patted the stack of rule books. Each one was about two inches thick. Half the class groaned. The other half was still staring at the speaker and hadn't seen the size of the new rule book.

Principal Buthaire continued, "We will be industrious. We will be compliant. We will set high, vigorous standards." And then a whole bunch of other boring stuff that made us all realize we were in deep doo doo. I instantly hated all the kids who had duct taped the former principal to the wall. Was it worth it, guys?

After we received Principal Buthaire's prison rules, we took attendance and then headed off to our classes. I had English and Math before meeting up with Ben in gym, where we were set to play every geek's favorite game, dodge ball.

Ben had the guts to ask Mr. Muscalini what the purpose of dodge ball was. Sometimes I wonder if the dude has a death wish. I know geeks don't like playing dodge ball, but there's really not much we can do about it other than hide behind other kids or take a few hits to the face for everyone else's viewing pleasure.

Mr. Muscalini couldn't even fathom that the idea that jocks throwing things at geeks as hard as they could was somehow a bad idea. He furrowed his brow as he stared down at Ben. "What's your name, son?" The glare, his deep voice and bulging muscles made it out to be a much more difficult question than it actually was.

Ben stammered, "Umm, Ben Gordon, sir?"

"Is that a question, Gordo?"

"No, sir. And it's Gordon." Ben straightened his shoulders and forced himself to look up into Mr. Muscalini's eyes.

Mr. Muscalini raised an eyebrow. "Let me tell you something, Gordo. Dodge ball is life. It's a part of the human condition. It's been around for thousands of years. It brings out our inner spirit. Our manhood!" He grabbed Ben by the shoulder as he animatedly described the geek-crushing game. "Cavemen and gladiators played the great game of dodge ball thousands of years ago. With rocks that could kill each other."

"That sounds...really scary."

"Nonsense. Squash the fear, Gordo. Unleash your inner caveman!" Mr. Muscalini flexed his bicep for effect and then admired it. Greatly.

"Sorry to interrupt, sir, but is that all?" Ben asked.

Mr. Muscalini finally looked away from his enormous bicep. "That depends on whether or not you have embraced the great game of dodge ball."

"I have, sir," Ben said as he nodded.

"I knew you had it in ya, Gordo," Mr. Muscalini said as he clapped Ben on the shoulder, nearly shattering his collar bone. "Try not to get killed out there."

Ben turned back to me, his eyes bulging. He whispered, "He's a nut job!"

Dodge ball went about as expected. My inner caveman was nowhere to be found. The only embracing that took place was geeks hugging in fear of getting crushed. It was horrifying. Ben took at least three hits to the face, while my butt had likely doubled in size from swelling. It was the worst 36 minutes of my life. And that's saying a lot with Derek Davenport as my brother.

I left the gym with less blood and self-esteem than when I entered, but I was still standing. Jason Parnell had to be wheeled down to the nurse's office in a wheelchair. And you know how kids are. By the end of the week, kids were saying that he nearly died and had to be medi-vacced to the hospital, not sure if they would be able to save his head. Which is not the kind of situation you want to be in, because last I checked, there's no such thing as a prosthetic head.

I hustled down the hall to swap out some books from my locker, Ben at my heels. My big butt cheeks didn't slow me down. I had planned out my route with precision and perfection. One swap after gym on the way to lunch and another after Spanish and I would be on time for all my classes. As I approached my locker, my mouth dropped open. My worst fear had been realized. Well, not really. My worst fear is getting eaten by an alligator. My second worst fear was getting Power Locked. I walked slowly toward my locker, my eyes focused on my padlock, which had been flipped backward and locked. The butt-chinned bandit had struck.

"Aaah, farts, man!" I said to no one in particular.

"Ooh, Power Locked. I think you just set the record for the earliest ever."

"Shut up, Ben." I love the kid, but sometimes he's flat-out unhelpful.

As I stared at Ben, my mind raced. Something beyond Ben caught my eye. A hulking man, at least six foot five, stared at me from down the hall as he leaned on a mop. Zorch.

"I'm gonna be late for lunch," I whined. "Who are we going to sit with?" I squatted down with my back to the locker and held out the lock, looking up at it.

"I'm sure we'll figure it out."

"Yeah, we're doing such a great job of that so far," I said sarcastically. I put in my combination and pulled the lock down. It jingled, but didn't pop open. "Come on." I tried it again. No luck.

"He must've switched out the lock. Maybe his. Do you know the combo?"

"If I knew the combo, it would be open."

"Okay, Mr. Cranky Pants. Calm down. Aww, nuts. Here comes Zorch."

"What?" I shrieked. This was the worst first day ever and it wasn't even close to over. I looked past Ben to see Zorch lumbering down the hall, his eyes locked on mine. He showed no emotion. He was Frankenstein without the scars. If I hadn't peed six times during dodge ball, I probably would've wet myself right there.

"Everything okay?" Zorch asked like a normal human being.

"I've had better days," I said.

Zorch reached for his belt and grabbed a ridiculously oversized ring of keys. I wasn't sure if he was a custodian or a dungeon master. Or both.

"Stand up," Zorch ordered.

I got off the ground and dusted myself off. Zorch found the key he was looking for and inserted it into the back of the lock. It popped open with a quick twist. He removed it and put it in his pocket. He reached into his other pocket and pulled out a lock with a tag on it. "Here's another one. The combo is on the tag."

I grabbed the lock. "Thank you, Zor...Um, what's your name, sir?" I asked as I looked up at his round, mustached face.

"Eugene, but the kids call me Zorch."

"Which do you prefer?"

He shrugged and thought about it for a second. "Nobody's really asked me that before. I guess I've grown to appreciate Zorch."

"Nice mustache, by the way, Zorch," Ben added. "Mine is coming in nicely." He rubbed his completely bald upper lip affectionately.

I popped the lock open and secured my locker before slipping my new combo into my pocket. I would commit it to memory and burn it as soon as possible. I couldn't risk another Power Lock.

"Thank you. You guys are alright."

"Right back atcha, Zorch. The gym floor is a dream," I called out as I took off down the hall. "Sorry if my blood is all over it," I said to myself.

Ben looked back at me as he ran. "We might actually make it on time." He disappeared around the corner.

I slid around the corner, making a wide turn and nearly

slammed into Ben's back. He stood at attention. A man with glasses and a clip-on tie with some sort of strange fish pattern glared down at us. It was the new principal. Uh, oh is right.

2

My heart pounded. I was not the type to get into trouble. My pulse quickened, meeting the pace of Principal Buthaire's rapidly-twitching eye. I was guessing he was more angry than nervous. Without saying a word, he began gesturing with his hands. I determined he was using sign language, but I was unclear as to why. Ben and I looked at each other for a moment before I gathered the courage to speak. "Umm, sir, I don't understand anything that you're saying."

"Oh. My apologies." Principal Buthaire feigned shock. "I thought you were both deaf."

"Why would you think that?" Ben blurted.

Principal Buthaire yelled so loud our hair blew back like we were hit by a tornado. A wet tornado. "Because I can't imagine why you would be in the hallway if you heard the bell ring!"

I was too shocked to answer. It was probably a good thing.

Principal Buthaire took a deep breath and straightened his fish tie. "Tardiness is a disease, Mr. Davenport."

I couldn't believe it. "How do you know my name?"

"I've been warned about you."

"About me? I think you mean my brother?"

"The genius?"

"That's me."

Principal Buthaire laughed uncontrollably. "You must be the funny one."

I shrugged. I do fancy myself entertaining from time to time. Principal Buthaire cut his laugh short and yelled, "I don't like jokes!" My career is not a joke and neither is your education. Got it, Jack?"

"Yes, sir."

The principal pulled out a pad, scribbled on it, tore it off, and handed it to me. "Detention slip." I grabbed it as he filled out a second one. "And your name is?"

"Benjamin Gordon."

Principal Buthaire tore the detention slip from the pad and handed it to Ben. "Get to where you need to be. Pronto." He stared at both of us and shook his head disapprovingly.

We speed walked down the hallway until we were out of Principal Buthaire's sight and then broken out into a jog to the cafeteria. We made our way to the back of the long lunch line. I hoped we could find two seats together in a nerd-safe zone. Well, you're never really safe in the cafeteria. The most you can hope for is a buffer of normal kids between you and the troublemakers. If they really want to get you, they will. Meatball Monday is usually that day.

"I already hate this place," I whispered to Ben in front of me on the line.

"Next year will be better. We won't be the low men on the totem pole," Ben said, trying to be encouraging.

"It's the first day!" I whisper shouted. "We're already giving up on the whole year?"

We stacked our trays with the most edible of foods. Stuff you can't mess up too badly. Grilled cheese is as easy as they come. Pudding is a definite. Bacon? Bring it. Fruit cocktail from a 55-gallon drum? It's a gamble. Chicken Cacciatore? That's a hard pass.

We paid the cashier and walked out into the cafeteria, my heart racing, as I held my breath. Standing side by side, we surveyed the rows of tables, looking for a friendly opening. My anxiety rose with each filled table.

"We're done for," Ben said.

"Ruined," I added.

And then we were both jolted out of our depression as some unknown kid approached, a smile on his face. "Hey guys!"

"Hi," I said curiously. Ben shifted from foot to foot, not sure of what to say or do.

The kid smiled as he inspected the food on our trays. "Grilled cheese. Yes. Oooh, chocolate milk. Cookies!" He gathered the items he enthusiastically mentioned and smiled. "See you tomorrow." The kid held up Ben's chocolate milk as if he was making a toast. "We're gonna have a great year!"

Yeah, spectacular. Ben looked at me, shaking his head. "Is it always going to be like this?"

I caught sight of my brother, Derek, sitting with all of the popular kids. "Pretty much. But what happened to next year will be better?" I asked.

"I'm not so sure anymore."

And then the real fun began. Well, for everyone else. Derek used his annoyingly-accurate arm to launch a handful of beef stroganoff across the cafeteria. I mean, who eats beef stroganoff? I guess that's not really that important. I froze as the beef, noodles, and cream hurdled toward me at warp speed. My cat-like reflexes kicked in just a second too late. Not only did my face take a direct hit of sticky noodles and rock-solid beef, I followed the stroganoff splattering with an awkward dive across the floor.

I skidded to a squeaky stop. What was left on my tray after it was raided, slid, splattered, and sprayed everyone within a five-foot radius. Ben caught the brunt of it. Laughter erupted like a volcano. I felt my face redden. I couldn't bear to look at anyone. I scrambled to my feet, nearly slipped and cracked my skull on random bits of stroganoff, and rushed out of the cafeteria. I was done with middle school. My mother was going to home school me. There was no other option.

Ben followed me into the hallway as I rushed toward the exit door. "Hey, whoa, wait!"

I ignored him and blasted the doors open with a Hulk-like force.

"What about Principal Buthaire?"

I really didn't care if a S.W.A.T. team was there armed and ready to send me back to class. I wasn't going. Principal Buthaire and his clip-on tie surely weren't going to stop me.

A voice asked me a strange question that shifted my angered state to, huh? "Want me to hose you down?"

I turned to see Zorch walking toward me. I sensed he was actually trying to be helpful and had already helped me once already, so I swallowed my snippy retort. The best I could do was ask, "Do you have kids?"

Zorch answered, "No. Not married. I have a dog."

And then it all made sense.

"Follow me," Zorch said with a wave.

I really didn't want to, but Zorch was not the kind of guy you said no to easily. Ben and I walked closely behind him. I looked at Ben who offered an unhelpful shrug. Zorch scanned a security card on a sensor outside a door. The door buzzed. Zorch grabbed it and pulled. We followed him into a large, packed room. We had been admitted entrance to Zorch's lair. Besides a small sitting area, the lair was filled with more janitorial supplies than Home Depot and Lowe's combined. Barrels of waxes and soaps were stacked to the ceiling. Mops, brooms, and poles with dusters lined the walls. I finally understood why my father always complained about how high the school taxes were.

Besides the supplies, there were crates of cut tennis balls, fidget spinners, and even some whoopie cushions lined in dust.

"What's your gym locker number?" Zorch asked.

"Umm, twenty one."

"I'll get your gym shirt. You can wash up back there." Zorch pointed to a faucet jutting from the wall above a rusty pail.

Not exactly luxury accommodations, but better than wearing beef stroganoff all day. By the time I got the last bit of creamy noodle off my face, Zorch had returned with my t-shirt from gym class.

I know I only wore it for one period, but it was for dodge ball. Running for your life generates a lot of sweat. Combine that with fear and you get one odiferous cocktail and a lot of disgusted classmates. I questioned whether or not I should just suck it up and smell like beef all day. Maybe chicks dug that. I was pretty certain that fear and body odor were not going to get me elected class president or a date to the Halloween dance. In the end, I still chose the gym shirt. The beef was changing colors. I don't know what they put in the sauce, but it was wearing off. Quickly.

Zorch nodded toward the clock on the wall. "Tick, tock."

"Thanks," I said to Zorch. He nodded.

"If we hurry, we can make the next class in time," Ben said.

"Lucky us," I muttered. If I didn't have science next, there was no way I would have even thought about staying another minute, let alone the rest of the day.

I entered the science lab just as the bell was ringing, perfect timing for someone trying to stay under the radar. The last thing I needed was peer ridicule and to relive the beef barrage. I slide into the closest seat at an empty lab table. And then a most unforeseen turn of events unfolded that changed my life. Two words. Soul. Mate. And Sophie. Rodriguez. So actually, four words. Well, five with the 'and'. Not as concise, but still, powerful.

I didn't know her name at the time, but when Sophie Rodriguez slipped into the seat next to me just after the bell, middle school became the greatest place on earth. There was something about her smile, her light blue eyes, and her brown, bouncy curls that made everything seem okay. I smiled back, glad she didn't say anything, because I wasn't certain I could even speak.

3

I pretty much ignored Sophie for the rest of the week, except when we had to interact for scientific purposes. I just didn't know what to say and she made me feel so nervous. I figured if I didn't talk, I couldn't mess things up. I almost talked with my butt a few times, but was able to hold it in until the bell rang. Thankfully, she was new to the school district and naturally on the quiet side, so I don't think the lack of talking (not from my butt) bothered her too much.

The first time we really talked about non-scientific things was Friday just before the bell rang to end class. Sophie was packing up her books and asked, "Will I see you at the fundraiser tomorrow?"

I thought for a moment about how to answer the question. Girls didn't usually wonder if they would see me places. At least not out loud. Unless she was trying to avoid me. "Do you want to?" I asked like an idiot.

Sophie laughed and furrowed her brow. "Yeah, you seem nice. Quiet, but nice. Maybe we can be on the same team."

I almost high-fived myself, but thought better of it. I

tried to hold in my giddiness. "That would be gre- very good."

She smiled. "Great. I'll see you in the morning."

I smiled like a doofus and waved as she walked out the door.

~

MY MOTHER DROVE Derek and me to the fundraiser. She was in the PTA and helped run the whole thing. It was a car wash in the back parking lot of the school. I wondered if we would even make a dent in Zorch's ridiculous hoard of soap.

Of course, my brother was his usual jerky self. "Why do we even have to do this? It's too early." He was probably up all night playing video games.

"The school budget doesn't cover all of the clubs and extra activities," my mother said, looking back at us through the rear-view mirror.

"We spend it all on janitorial supplies," I added.

"You're such a dork. The only kid who studies the school budget."

"Derek-" my mother said.

I looked at Derek and smirked. "I was joking, but I guess with your limited intellect, you didn't get it."

"Or you're just not funny."

"Boys, enough."

"Why does the football team get new uniforms, but we have to raise money for the science club?" I asked.

"I don't know, honey."

"Football's cooler than science," Derek said.

I rolled my eyes as we pulled into the parking lot. I stuck to my usual plan when I got out of the car, which was to get as far away from Derek as possible. I smiled when I saw Ben approaching and Derek veering off toward Jayden Johnson, his best friend. I searched the various packs of helpers hoping to find Sophie. I had thought about it all night and I was going to try to talk to her.

I looked all around, but Sophie was nowhere to be found. I was half disappointed, half relieved. If she wasn't there, I couldn't embarrass myself or be embarrassed in front of her. I ended up in a group of three with Ben and Luke Hill, a nice kid I went to elementary school with. We had a lot of fun and even washed a few cars. Ben cleaned Luke's crew-cutted head with a soapy sponge and I crafted a massive bubble beard for myself.

The bubble beard seemed like a great idea at the time, until I felt a tap on my shoulder. I thought it was going to be my mother telling me to knock it off and wash some cars, but it was far worse. I turned around with my Santa beard and said, "Hey, Momma. Your baby boy is all grown..." My eyes met Sophie's and then I crumpled to the ground in a heap of humiliation, started sucking my thumb, and died. The End.

At least it felt like death. And then I heard the sweetest sound. Sophie laughed. I opened my eyes, curious to understand her reaction and why I was still alive. "I like it. You should grow it out more."

I got lost in her dimples and smile. It was a glorious adventure. One that I didn't want to end, but unfortunately did with a massive blast to the face of cold water. I gasped for air as the pummeling not only demolished my fab bubble beard, but my ego as well. I turned away from the stream of water and wiped my eyes, my hair and face sopping wet. I was surrounded by laughter.

I didn't need to ask who it was. I wasn't surprised when I heard Ben say, "Derek, you're such an idiot."

I continued to wipe my face with my wet hands, which was not my best ever idea, but the best I could do at that moment. I ran my fingers through my hair, hoping that it would at least look lit, wet and slicked back.

I wanted to run, but they would've made fun about how I ran, too, so I turned and glared at Derek, who continued to laugh with his gang of dumb friends. Ben, Luke, and Sophie surrounded me and attempted to cheer me up.

"Don't worry about it," Luke said.

I was still mad. "Easy for you to say. It didn't happen to you in front of Soph-" I caught myself, but I wasn't sure if it was too late or not. "In front of the whole school," I corrected. I looked at Sophie, but didn't know if she knew I was talking about her.

"Everybody knows Derek is a jerk," Ben said.

Sophie rubbed my arm. "Anyone who laughed isn't worth being friends with anyway."

"Yeah, but my brother isn't going anywhere."

Nobody had a good response to that. I walked away, leaving them behind, and plopped down on the grass in front of our car until the fundraiser was over. I just wanted to be alone.

~

I WAS PRETTY quiet at dinner. We sat at a round table in our kitchen, all five of us: my parents; Derek; my high-school sister, Leighton; and me. Roast beef and mashed potatoes. I picked at my food. I was still on the outs with beef in general, even though there were no noodles or cream on my plate. I was still annoyed about the cafeteria and the fundraiser, tired of my brother embarrassing me. And the fact that he embarrassed me in front of Sophie made it that much worse.

My mother attempted to make some conversation. "I'm on the Halloween dance committee. Will either of you be asking anyone as a date?"

Sophie immediately came to mind. It would make my life to have her as my date. I just didn't think she would actually say yes. As I thought about whether or not I should share any of this with my family, Derek answered, "I'm going to ask Sophie Rodriguez. She's in my art class."

It took a moment for it all to register. And then my heart imploded and my soul disintegrated into a million tear-drop shaped pieces. Luckily, I hadn't eaten too much or else I would've up chucked it all across the table at my sister's face. I was frozen. I couldn't move.

"Austin. Austin!" My mother shook my arm. "Are you okay?"

I snapped out of the stupor I was in and nodded. "Yeah, yep, absolutely. I, umm, I'm not asking anyone."

"What a dork," Derek whispered under his breath.

I stared at my mashed potatoes, fuming. I looked over at my brother next to me, my eyes boring into him as he looked down at his plate. I scooped up a handful of it and chucked it at his face. I yelled, "I hate you! Don't ever speak to me again." I was sure I would pay for it in the future, but it was worth it.

All five of us were shocked. Not only because of what I tried to do, but what I actually succeeded in doing. Normally, when going up against Derek, I lose badly. I stormed off to my room before my parents could regain their composure and send me there anyway.

4

Thankfully, I had my own bedroom. My parents at least knew that I needed a safe place away from Darth Derek. You can call him Derek the Destroyer if you like that better. I tried to watch TV, but I was too angry to enjoy any of it. I clicked the power button on the remote and tossed it across the room. I spent most of Saturday night in a semi-comatose state watching the ceiling fan whir around and around. I should've kept count. I probably would've set a Guinness World Record.

I woke up Sunday morning to a knock at my door. I grabbed my pillow and covered my head with it. I hoped whomever it was would go away. No luck. It's kinda my thing. The knocking continued. I reluctantly responded, "Who is it?" I hoped it wasn't Derek attempting to make a poor excuse of an apology. I lost count of how many times he promised not to be a jerk and then was a jerk.

But thankfully, my mother answered, "It's me, honey. Can I come in?"

"Can I say no?" I mumbled through the pillow.

"No."

"Well, then, it's open."

The door opened slowly. I sat up on my bed. "I'm not apologizing to him."

"I didn't ask you to. I just wanted to make sure you're alright."

"I'm not. I don't know if I will ever be. Why does he treat me that way? Why is my life so unfair?" I had more questions, but I was trying not to cry.

"I don't know why he does that. He feels really bad about it."

"No, he doesn't. He's very good at pretending he feels bad about it. The next opportunity, he'll find a way to embarrass me again. If this was just some random kid at school, you would be going nuts, but because it's your favorite son, Derek, you pretend like it's just boys being boys. Get out."

"Honey-"

"Get out!"

I spent the rest of the day alone in my room. My only contact with the outside world was a few FaceTime sessions with Ben. Both my parents tried to talk to me, but I refused to talk and eventually fell asleep after everyone left me alone.

～

MONDAY MORNING CAME WAY TOO QUICKLY. My alarm rang. It felt like a brick fell on my head. I never hit the snooze button, but I did that morning, which meant I lost to Derek in one of the only things I could beat him in, waking up earlier and being first to the bathroom. I know, sometimes I even amaze myself with my talents.

I lumbered to the bathroom and twisted the handle.

Locked. I heard footsteps. I turned around and was able to make out that the Wookie headed toward me was actually my sister.

"Ugh, I'm going to be late," she whined.

"Me, too." I slapped the door. "Let's go. Get your hustle on."

After a few moments, my sister pushed me aside. "What are you doing in there?"

"Chill! I'm combing my mustache!" Derek yelled.

"Are you serious?" Leighton asked, annoyed.

"It's peach fuzz," I added.

"Is not. You don't condition peach fuzz," Derek said.

"You conditioned your 'mustache'?" My sister asked, laughing.

I was not enthused. "Grandma's mustache is thicker than yours. Get out of the bathroom, Derek."

"Grandma's mustache is thicker than a lot of mustaches. It doesn't mean there's anything wrong with mine. This is the deal sealer," Derek said, much more confident than he should have.

"What is he talking about?" Leighton asked me.

I shrugged.

"Sophie loves it. She stares at it all the time."

I just turned and walked away. Morning hygiene was overrated, anyway.

∾

THE SCHOOL MORNING WAS UNEVENTFUL, at least until I had to go to the bathroom. Badly. If there is anything that has the potential to be eventful, it's going to the bathroom in middle school. I sat in the front of Dr. Dinkledorf's classroom considering my options. I crossed my legs tight, but it didn't seem to help. I know it sounds like an easy solution would be to actually go to the bathroom. The problem was that I was in the east wing. The east wing bathroom was private. Yes, there was a private bathroom in my public middle school, run by Max Mulvihill. I'll explain more later, but all you need to know now is that I wasn't a member. My only other option was to make a run for the west wing bathroom and if I didn't make it, stop off at the nurse and get a pair of sweatpants from the nurse. After the beef stroganoff and car wash incidents, peeing in my pants wasn't going to hurt my reputation all that much. I was no doubt in last place in the cool contest already.

I reached into my pocket to stop the change from jingling, as I was getting antsy. My fingers grabbed a crumpled up ball of paper. I pulled it out to find it was three dollar bills. My brain amped up into high gear. My options just improved a fair amount. I was going to haggle with Max Mulvihill. With no time to spare before my bladder burst like a firecracker, I raised my hand and blurted out, "Dr. Dinkledorf, can I go to the bathroom?"

Some idiot in the back called out, "Right here?" A few chuckles ensued.

Dr. Dinkledorf nodded as he continued his history lesson. I darted out of the chair, grabbed the pass hanging next to the door, and rushed out of the class toward the bathroom. I was careful to listen for other footsteps to avoid getting in trouble for running in the hallways by our new principal/warden. I made it there without any issues.

I took a deep breath and pushed open the door. The bathroom in the east wing is pretty much off limits except for the bullies and rich kids. Max Mulvihill seemingly lives there and charges a cover for entry, or so I've heard. I think the rich kids just assumed that the school provided a bathroom attendant. He does offer mints and cheap cologne if you visit his fine establishment. I'm not sure why Zorch allows it. My guess is that he gets a cut of Max's revenue. His car, the Zorchmobile, as it is affectionately known, is way too nice for him not to be in on the deal.

Max Mulvihill stood up from a leather chair and walked over to me. He was at least a foot taller and fifty pounds heavier than I was. He looked at me, his eyebrow raised. I smiled and said, "Just need to use the bathroom." I attempted to walk past him, but he slid over blocking my path.

"Who are you?"

"Austin Davenport."

"Sorry. This is a private establishment. It's five dollars a visit. Or you can use the free one over by the west wing."

"I'll give you a dollar. I just have to pee." I tried not to seem too antsy. The worse I had to go, the less negotiating leverage I had.

"Five. What are you doing with your legs there?" He looked down at the tiny quiver in my knees.

"Nothing. I'm fine," I lied.

"Water. Flowing bath water. Niagara Falls gushing."

I started to fidget a little bit. I was losing, but he didn't counter my original offer. "Two dollars."

"Five."

"I don't have to poop. Three dollars or I'm going to the gym locker room."

"That's a mighty far trek. Not sure you'll make it."

"My mother keeps clothes for me at the nurse. I'll pee myself before I pay you five."

"If I lower the price for you, it could hurt my business. I don't need everyone asking for discounts."

"I won't tell anyone. I swear. I'll even dare my brother to

flood the gym bathroom- you'll get half the school's business."

Max thought it over for a moment. It felt like a year. My insides were being stretched beyond human capability. May Day. May Day. I couldn't wait for an answer. "I'll give you the three now and if my brother doesn't flood the bathroom, I'll pay you another five."

"For three dollars, you don't get a beverage or the artisanal cheeses."

"Fair enough," I blurted out.

"You drive a hard bargain, Davenport. Welcome to the east wing lounge." Max stepped aside as I rushed toward a stall and blasted the door open. It was the best pee of my life. I don't keep a journal or any type of accounting, but I'm pretty certain of it.

Once I was done, I went to wash my hands. I had a chance to check out Max's operation. The place was unreal. He had four different cheap colognes, a disco ball, a pinball machine, a fridge, and a massage chair that I think he stole from the mall. I'm sure he charged extra for that.

I nodded to him on the way out and said, "Thanks."

"See you later, ladies' man!"

Ladies' man? What the heck was he talking about?

A fter the bell rang, I left Dr. Dinkledorf's class and headed upstairs. A bunch of people pointed at me, laughing. I wasn't sure for what. I had a pretty long list in just under a week at the place. I didn't know for certain what it was until someone said, "Nice video."

"What video?" I asked. The kid chuckled with his friends, ignored me, and kept on walking.

Maggie Pruitt heard my question and stopped. "You don't know?"

I shrugged. Anxiety pulsed through my veins. "Just tell me."

"I'm sorry, Austin. I'll show you." Maggie pulled out her phone, opened Snapchat, and played a video of me taken on the bus. I closed my eyes, knowing exactly what it was going to show: me talking to Ben about Sophie.

And then I heard my voice say, "Does Sophie Davenport sound good?"

"Did my brother post it?" I asked after a deep breath.

"No. Somebody I never heard of. Justin Larson?"

"Never heard of him." I shook my head. "Thanks, Maggie."

"Sorry," she said, sheepishly.

"Me, too." I continued on my way to class, ignoring everyone.

I spent the rest of the day in hiberfrustration, which is a state where one is so frustrated, they shut down and shut out the outside world. I couldn't handle any more negativity, so I closed up shop for the day. Until I got home. That's when I unleashed the beast. I waited until my father was nearby to break up the fight I was about to start with Derek. I was angry, but not stupid.

"Hey, butt face!" I yelled at Derek. He wasn't in a sound-proof room or anything.

Derek and my father both looked at me, confused.

"Yeah, I'm talking to you, Derek. I know you had something to do with that video today."

"I don't know what you're talking about."

I knew he would deny it, but it still made me angry. I rushed him and pushed him in the chest. He took two steps back and thrust his hands at my shoulders. I tried to slap them away, but the force was too strong, and I slammed back into the wall. The picture frames shook.

"Hey, whoa! What's going on?" My father skidded in between us.

"He took a video of me on the bus and posted it on Snapchat!"

"Derek, is this true?"

"No. I don't know what he's talking about. Check my phone."

My dad looked at me. "Did you see the video?"

"Yeah."

"Who posted it?"

"Some kid I never heard of."

"So why are you blaming me?" Derek asked.

"Because I know you had something to do with it. Who took the video on the bus?"

"I don't know. I had nothing to do with it." Derek shrugged his shoulders at my father. "I swear."

"You're such a liar. First the food fight, then the hose, now this. You make me sick. I wish I was never born. Actually, correction. I wish you were never born."

"Austin!" my father yelled. "Apologize!"

"Yeah, take his side, as always. I'm sick of this family." I stormed out of the room, knocking a pile of mail on the floor. I showed it who was boss.

I decided I was going to ask Sophie to the dance before Derek did. She would probably say no, but I was used to losing to him. I just needed to occupy Derek so he would forget about Sophie, or at least not rush to ask her out.

~

As I HOPPED off the bus the next morning with Ben at my side, I waited for my brother to catch up. He stared at me confused. I shook my head. "I don't know why I care, because I still hate you, but somebody told me you were going to flood the bathroom next to the gym? That's a bad idea."

"I wasn't planning on it, but," Derek said as he shrugged.

"I don't think you could even pull it off. Too hard with Zorch everywhere and the new principal."

"I'm intrigued. I could think of worse things to do. Maybe I'll do those, too."

6

I was sick to my stomach. I hadn't seen Sophie since the video went viral around Cherry Avenue. I hoped she hadn't seen it since she was new to the district. I wasn't sure how to handle it. Should I just tell her how I felt and ask her to the dance? Should I try to play it like nothing happened and see if she says anything about it? Should I claim I was tricked? Or should I never show up to science again?

I decided on never showing up to science again. Well, at least for that day. I cut my first class ever and walked across the school grounds to see if I could find my sister. I needed advice and I knew she hung out outside during lunch.

I walked around the corner of the school and into the courtyard. I got a few curious looks from some high school kids, but most didn't pay me any attention. I searched the small packs of kids and finally found Leighton. She pretended she didn't see me, but quickly realized she couldn't avoid me as I waved to her from across the court-yard, which only drew more attention to her.

She grabbed me by the shoulder and pushed me

behind a wall of her friends. "What are you doing here? Tucker Allen is about to ask me to the homecoming dance."

"Okay?" I said, not sure why that was important to me.

"As a freshman. He's a senior."

"It's good to see you, too, sis."

Leighton eased up a little. "What's the matter? Something wrong?"

"I need help."

"No."

"You don't even know what I need help with! You want me to tell Tucker Allen about your back hair?'

"I don't have back hair."

"He doesn't know that." I shrugged, calmly.

"You wouldn't!"

"Then help me. If I win, it will make Derek look like an idiot." I should've just led with that.

My sister said enthusiastically, "What do you need?"

Leighton's friend, Becky Tisdale, chimed in. "We're taking down Derek? I'm in."

"I need to get Sophie Rodriguez to go to the Halloween dance with me."

"Does she know you?" my sister asked.

"Yes. Am I that pathetic?" I asked before realizing I didn't want her to answer.

"Compliment her. Just be nice. You're good at that," Leighton said.

Becky shook her head. "No, you gotta act tough. Be a bad boy."

"Do I look like the bad boy type?"

"Not...particularly, no," Becky said, carefully.

I grunted. "This is a waste. She's not going to say yes anyway."

"Don't say that," Leighton said. "What does Dad always say?"

"Shut up and go to bed?"

"I don't see how that helps here, Leigh," Becky said tapping her chin.

"No, he always says, 'Life is about showing up.' For me, I almost quit soccer, because I didn't think I was good enough to make the school team. He told me not to cut myself from the team. If the coach didn't think I was good enough, that was okay, but I shouldn't not try."

I nodded, soaking it in. "I think I got it. Thanks, sis." I smiled at her, as I turned to walk back to school.

"Go get 'em, tiger," Leighton said and smiled back at me.

"Don't not try!" Becky said. I never said she was my sister's smartest friend.

I snuck back into school in between classes while kids were in transit. I felt bad about cutting science. I loved science and Mr. Gifford. He liked my sister when she had him, so we bonded a little bit. I hoped he wouldn't be disappointed. I found out the answer very quickly. Heading to my next class, I saw him across the hall. It was hard to miss him. He was almost a foot and a half taller than all the kids. I ducked behind Kieran Murphy, but Mr. Gifford spotted me.

"Mister Davenport, I missed you in class." He stared at me, waiting for me to respond.

"I missed you, too, sir. I'll see you tomorrow, though." I smiled, hoping that would suffice, and starting walking again.

"Not so fast. Why weren't you in class?"

I stopped and looked up at him. "I'm really sorry. I needed to see my sister. I've been having a tough time with my brother. And there's this girl we both like and I want to go to the dance with her, and-"

He put his hand on my shoulder. "Say no more. I'm not going to turn you in for cutting. I've had girl problems, too. Did she have any good advice?" Mr. Gifford asked a little too desperately.

"You gotta show up."

"Indeed you do," Mr. Gifford said, nodding. "Do you think I should get a tattoo so the ladies think I'm a bad boy?"

I looked at his suspenders and pursed my lips. "No. You're more the intellectual type. Wear a turtleneck. Grow a beard. Maybe get a tweed jacket with suede elbow patches."

"You're a genius, Austin! I'm going to upgrade my dating profile pic immediately!"

"Sir, you should probably grow the beard first and go shopping."

"Right. That's an excellent point."

I gave Mr. Gifford a thumbs up. "Okay then. We're good here? I'll see you tomorrow."

He pointed his finger at me and winked. "You'll see me unshaven."

"Looking forward to it, sir."

∽

THE NEXT TWENTY-THREE hours were torturous. I couldn't decide how or when to ask Sophie to the dance. I was afraid I might see her in the halls and not know what to say. After school, I wondered if I should just call her and her ask over the phone. That way if she turned me down, she wouldn't see my tears. As the night ticked on, I didn't know what to say if I did call her, so I didn't. 'Do you want to go to the dance with me?' wasn't good enough. It had the unoriginality of my brother. But what?

I was at a loss. I wanted to talk to my sister, but she was

FaceTiming, Snapchatting, and texting with every device, finger, and toe she owned. Tucker Allen asked her to the dance. She kept waving me away every time I opened her door. All I needed to know was what he said when he asked!

I walked into science class no more prepared than when I decided to ask Sophie to the dance. I sat down next to her. It was awkward, because even though the bell rang, Mr. Gifford refused to start teaching. He won't speak a word of educational information until the entire room is quiet, which given his old age, often has me concerned that he's going to turn into a skeleton before we actually learn anything. Rumor has it that the skeleton in the science lab is Mr. Jenkins, who used to teach here and had similar rules.

Mrs. Conklin, my English teacher, is the exact opposite. She doesn't care if kids are swinging from the chandeliers (we have a really nice middle school) or if the place is on fire. She's got a lesson plan and she sticks to it. Nobody has any idea what's she's saying half the time, but I admire her persistence.

Anyway, back to the awkwardness. I doodled on my notebook and tried to steal a few glances at Sophie to see if she suspected anything. Suspect what, I didn't know. I learned nothing, other than that I'm not a very good detective. Finally and thankfully, Mr. Gifford started teaching.

"Okay, class. As I mentioned yesterday, today's lab is on organic versus chemically-fertilized plant growth. Put on your gloves and goggles and then pick up your soil and fertilizer."

I put on my gloves and looked over at Sophie. I had to make my move before I put on those ridiculous goggles. They weren't going to help. At all. I still had no idea what to say! I guess I was staring at her because she looked at me with her goggles on and said, "Are you okay?"

"Yes, I umm, was just thinking about how beautiful you look in goggles." What an idiot I am. And I wasn't done. "They match your dress nicely."

Sophie laughed. "They're clear. They match everything, but thank you."

I smiled, relieved that she laughed. And that I didn't pee down my leg. I didn't care that I hadn't asked about the dance yet.

"Why weren't you in class yesterday? I saw you in the morning."

"I was..." I thought about lying. I was sick or dead even, but I decided to tell the truth. "I don't know if you saw it, but I was embarrassed about a video that went around about me. If you haven't seen it, please don't watch it." I held my breath waiting for her response.

"I liked it. It was sweet. You're sweet." Sophie looked at me shyly.

I didn't know what to say. My heart was racing. I wanted to run through the halls screaming and thanking the Big Man upstairs. And then I smelled something horrifying. There was a chance I had somehow just pooped in my pants. After analyzing the situation, I knew it wasn't me.

And then I saw half the class smelling the organic fertilizer and complaining about how gross it was.

"Are you okay?" Sophie asked.

I smiled. "Never better." I looked around the room as the rest of the class was getting started on the lab project. "We better get going."

"Right," Sophie agreed. "I'll get the fertilizer."

Sophie and I completed our lab with the minimum amount of interaction. I wanted to ask her to the dance, but I couldn't summon up the courage. My mind was so focused on psyching myself up that I didn't say much of anything to her.

As we were cleaning up the lab, Sophie asked, "Do you have a phone?"

I pulled my phone out of my backpack.

"Can I borrow it?"

"Yeah," I said, as I put in my password. I handed it to her.

Sophie opened up my contacts and started typing. "This is my number. Text me. We can study for the quiz together." She handed the phone back to me.

I looked down at the number and back up at Sophie. And then again. I was shocked. "This kinda looks like the Chinese takeout number."

"It's not," she chuckled. "It's the pizza place."

"That's not Frank's Pizza."

"I was talking about Lombardi's."

"Nobody eats at Lombardi's. Frank's is so much better."

"Wow." Sophie feigned anger. "Never insult a girl's pizza place, but maybe you can take me to Frank's some time. See you later." Sophie laughed, as she turned to walk out.

I nodded, still not believing what had just happened.

7

That night as I lay in my bed, my huge analytical mind assessed every angle of the day's events. There was only one conclusion, impossible as it seemed to be. Sophie liked me. But why? My huge analytical mind had yet to figure that out. I had barely spoken to her up until that point. I had enough to worry about in my middle school experience that I decided to let it be, misguided as she may be. I deserved a little bit of luck. I went to bed with confidence. The next day was my day. I was going to ask Sophie to the dance.

That next morning was a perfect day with clear blue skies and sunny, but not too hot. Mr. Muscalini decided to ruin it by bringing the class outside onto the track for some running and relay races. It was at that moment that I learned that Sophie had gym during the same period and the girls would be joining us.

My anxiety was off the charts. I looked over at Ben as we walked around the track during our warm up. "What do I do?"

"You gotta go for it before Derek messes it up. Or you mess it up once she sees you run."

I nodded. "Good point. I'm just gonna do it." I pumped my fists. "I gotta do it!" I looked over across the track and eyed Sophie stretching by the bleachers. "I'm just gonna ask her right now. I can do this!"

""You got this, man! You're The Rock! You're Luke Skywalker! You're a Jedi! The force is strong with this one!"

I looked over at Ben. "Yo dude, chill out on the soda for breakfast."

Ben shrugged. As we got closer to the bleachers, Mr. Muscalini yelled, "Let's go! Men don't walk the track! They run!"

I huffed, but started running. The bleachers were rapidly approaching. The girls were about to hit the track, too. Sophie was only a few lanes away from me, so I was going to run right by her. She was so beautiful. Even her ear lobes were cute. Sophie waved at me. I stared at her.

Ben elbowed me in the stomach. "Wave back, idiot!"

I shook the cobwebs out of my head and waved back with a goofy grin on my face. I passed by, completely forgetting to ask her to the dance! I had a whole other lap to run before I could ask her, which was a lot of time for things to go wrong. Things go wrong when nerds run. I made sure to lift my knees up and watch where I was going to avoid any potholes, rocks, or painted lines that could trip me up. Ben was trying to pump me up, but I blocked him out. I still didn't know what to say.

Sophie stretched on the track as I steeled my eyes on her, hoping that somehow she would tell me what to say. My mental telepathy skills failed me terribly. Only a hundred feet away, I had nothing, and the girls, about to start walking, were congregating in bigger groups on the track. Whatever I said to Sophie would be heard by, well, all of them. I gulped. My heart rate and sweat rate accelerated.

I edged closer to her because I didn't want to scream, but I did have to yell it as I passed by because Mr. Muscalini was watching. Dread overtook me. What if she said no?

Ben shook me out of my doubt with another elbow and said, "Now!" like I was pushing the button on a nuclear device or something.

Jolted by his elbow, I didn't have a chance to think, only a few steps away from Sophie. I blurted, "Do you want to go to the Halloween dance?"

Sophie smiled and said, "Yes."

My heart leapt, but then I quickly realized I left out a key detail. I turned and looked back at her. "I mean with me?"

"I'd love to!"

I wasn't sure I heard her correctly. "Really?" And then stepped on Ben's foot and fell flat on my face. Smooth. I look at it as a positive. I got some kissing practice in. True, it was hot asphalt, but I am better prepared than before the fall.

8

E ven though the fall hurt, it was nothing compared to the excitement that I felt knowing Sophie wanted to go to the Halloween dance with me. After receiving minor medical attention, I did actually confirm that Sophie really meant she wanted to go with me.

I spent most of the rest of the day in awe that it had actually happened and wondering when was too soon to text her.

I stood outside Ben's locker as he searched for a notebook in his already-messy locker. "Just text her," Ben said, the sound echoing inside his locker.

"How do you know? You've never had a girlfriend."

"She's your girlfriend now? And if she is, you wouldn't have her if it wasn't for me." Ben grabbed the book and slammed his locker.

"I don't know. And you're right. Where should I text her? I don't want my phone to get taken away."

And then my phone dinged. I slid it out of my backpack and stared at it, my mouth wide open. Sophie texted me!

It read, 'How's your face?'

Ben looked over at it. "What do I do?" I asked frantically.

"Tell her how your face is," Ben said. He may have added a 'duh', but I won't confirm that.

I answered, 'Good. How's yours?'

"How's yours?" Ben looked up at the ceiling, shaking his head.

"What? It's rude not to ask."

Ben took a deep breath. "I've lost all hope..."

I looked at my phone as we walked down the hallway. She was typing me back, but I will never know what she said, because my phone was viciously and anti-Americanly ripped from my hand by one Principal Buthaire.

"Mr. Davenport, so lovely to see you on this fine afternoon."

He pretended to be nice, but based on the phone-ripping, I knew I was toast.

"I'm sorry for texting, sir, but it was an emergency." I held my breath, hoping he would believe me and return my phone.

"Oh, okay. No problem. Let me just see here." Principal Buthaire looked at my phone. "How's your face? Good, how's yours?" He glared at me. "Should I dial 9-1-1? Or did Mr. Gordon already do that for you?"

"I meant more that it was important..." I said, as I reluctantly grabbed the detention slip.

"I will hold onto this until the end of the day." Principal Buthaire tucked my phone inside his suit jacket. "You can pick it up in my office."

"Yes, sir."

∾

I SAT at the edge of my seat throughout eighth period, waiting for the bell to ring, so I could get my phone and continue texting Sophie. I counted down the minutes. Only one to go. And then I heard the loudspeaker crackle. "Good afternoon, Cherry Avenue Gophers," Principal Buthaire said as if he really was not bidding us a good afternoon. And yes, our mascot is the fearsome gopher. Don't mess with us. We come from Cherry Avenue.

Anyway, our principal continued, "I have instituted a new rule. Any texting during school hours, whether it is in class or in the halls between classes, will result in detention. Courtesy of Austin Davenport. Be sure to thank him." He then wished us a "Good afternoon," with much greater enthusiasm than the first.

I looked over at the rest of my class and saw a lot of angry faces. I forced a nervous smile. "I don't know what he's talking about."

As the bell rang, I darted from my desk, dodging crumpled up pieces of paper, chalkboard erasers, and somebody's shoe. Dodge ball in gym class actually paid off. However, I couldn't dodge the insults. They still sting to this day.

Despite being public enemy number one, Sophie still wanted to go to the dance with me, so I was still riding high. The problem was that I drank too much Yoohoo celebrating with Ben at lunch that I had to pee. And I was in the east wing again, which meant a visit to Max Mulvihill. The whole thing burned me up. I mean, who was this guy preying on the small bladders of children? I'm all for capitalism, but Mulvihill was pushing it.

I pushed the door in, angry at myself for overdoing the Yoohoo, which was going to cost me five bucks. Max met me at the door. "Oh, it's you. Need to buy a burner phone?"

"What?"

"I can hook you up with an untraceable cell phone. If it gets confiscated, no big deal."

"Good to know, but I just have to pee."

"Well, we have a little problem, don't we?"

"What's that?" I pretended I didn't know what he was talking about.

"You owe me money. You don't go when you owe."

"I'm still working on the flooding issue. My brother is very intrigued by the opportunity."

"I can't take my girl to the movies on intrigue, bro."

"You have kids?"

"My girlfriend, dude."

"Honest mistake. You're very mature." To be honest, I wasn't sure how old he was. Based on this facial hair, I was thinking mid-twenties, but my mother always told me it was rude to ask an adult's age. I guess that still applies when you're not sure if the person is actually an adult or not.

"Perhaps we can barter."

"I did that and you didn't deliver."

"I will offer you my consulting services. If my idea is worthy, you let me pee. If not, I will take my business elsewhere."

"Okay, hot shot. What'dya got?" Max crossed his arms, unconvinced of my business acumen.

I stood next to Max and put my hand on his shoulder. "Two words," I said as I pretended the two words were on a giant billboard. "Sustainable revenue."

"Hmm," Max said.

I continued, "Right now, you never know when people are going to stop by. They don't want to pay every time. If they have any other option, they're not coming here."

"It *is* a challenge having competition give their services away for free," Max said, starting to see things my way.

"If you have a subscription model, they pay monthly for unlimited flushage or give them five poos for a discount. Maybe have a customer loyalty program."

"Yeah, but if I do that, I give up my leverage. You know how much money I make when a stomach bug is going around?"

"I hear you, but do you really want to have to sell your product every time someone walks in the door? You might not be able to squeeze every last penny out of them during flu season, but you know every month, the business is coming in the door. They may eat a little more of the artisanal cheeses, but you can manage that."

"That's not a big deal. I steal those anyway." Max paced around the bathroom, considering my points. I waited patiently, hoping my bladder would join me. "Davenport, you're a good man. I'll tell you what. Help me revamp my business plan and you can pee here for free anytime."

"Dude, thank you."

"Still gotta pay to poop!"

"Of course...that's a given." Things were looking up.

Well, at least I thought they were. Little did I know that my Halloween dance victory would spur my brother to make a vow to end the budding relationship between Sophie and me, or Saustin, as we were quickly and affectionately becoming known as. I hoped it had nothing to do with the beef stroganoff incident.

9

I headed to school with a bit of swagger in my step. I wasn't wearing sunglasses and didn't have my collar up like the cool kids, but there was a bounce in my step that I never had before and a little bit of a head bob if I'm being honest. My brother even handed my school bag to me as we headed out the door to catch the bus. I guess I earned his respect.

The morning got infinitely better from there.

Ben and Sammie rushed up to me in the hallway on the way to Math, smiles from ear to ear.

"Have you heard?" Sammie asked.

"There's no way, he's heard. Look at his face," Ben pointed at my face.

"What's wrong with my face?" Was it still scratched up from my make out session with the track?

"You're not smiling like we are," Ben said.

"Okay. So tell me." I was excited.

Sammie stepped in and whispered excitedly, "Somebody snuck into Principal Buthaire's office and put baby powder in his fan."

"Yeah, and when he got in this morning, he leaned over it to turn it on. It blew it all right onto his face. Mustache! Glasses! Covered!"

"It was like a volcanic explosion! You should've been there!" Sammie yelled.

"You saw it?" I asked, excitedly.

"Well, no, but everybody's talking about it," Sammie said.

"Still, that's awesome!" I said. "Who do you think did it?"

"Nobody knows, but he's a hero," Ben answered.

"Or she," Sammie corrected, annoyed.

"Ok. Thanks, guys. I gotta go. But great news!" I gave them a thumbs up and headed to class.

The bounce in my step as I headed off to class was noticeably bigger, the head bob more pronounced, and I may have even added pursed lips and a spin move when the situation called for it. It was my morning.

The afternoon? Not mine. Not at all. Swagger gone. Bounce flattened. Head bob? Nowhere to be found.

As I walked to Spanish, I heard the loathsome voice of Principal Buthaire call out from behind me, "Oh, Mr. Davenport? May I have a word?"

I turned to see a smirk peeking out from beneath his mustache.

"A little birdie told me you and I should chat."

I took a deep breath and closed my eyes for a split second, praying for patience. Turns out, I didn't receive any. "Was it the little birdie on your clip-on tie? Because, sir, if you're talking to your tie, you should see someone about that."

Principal Buthaire rolled his eyes. "I don't understand what your teachers see in you."

"That's very constructive of you. Thank you for your kind words. Can I go now?"

"No!" he yelled.

My shoulders slumped.

"Is your bag heavy?" Professor Buthaire asked. It was an odd question, so I was instantly concerned, not knowing what he was getting at.

"No."

"I assume you heard of the prank that was played on me today?" Principal Buthaire raised an eyebrow.

"Yes, the baby powder. Unfortunate." Unfortunate that I didn't see it happen. I would've paid to see it in slow motion, the powder blasting his mustache and coating his glasses. Principal Buthaire coughing and then raging. It must've been legendary. Much props to whomever accomplished that. And then it turned out it was me.

"Remember that little birdie I mentioned? It sang like a canary. And told me you're the perpetrator! Now give me that backpack!" Principal Buthaire ripped the backpack off my shoulder and tore it open.

I stood there horrified, not sure of what to say. Principal Buthaire rifled through my bag, emptying all of its contents onto the floor. He smiled as he dropped the bag to the floor, clutching a small, black plastic bag with something wrapped inside. He opened the bag and pulled out a white container of baby powder. Principal Buthaire laughed an evil cackle of a laugh. I think I may have heard thunder and seen lighting flash off in the distance.

My heart sunk. I knew I was in trouble. "That's not mine." I racked my brain trying to figure out where it came from. Given the fear I had of suspension or even worse, expulsion from school entirely, I couldn't think.

"That's what they all say, Mr. Davenport. You are to serve one week in in-school suspension and receive a mark on your permanent record!" I'd never seen him so happy. My parents, not so much.

10

I was grounded for two weeks. Me! I'm the angel of the family. I mean, it's not hard when you have a teenage sister and Derek for a brother, but still. I'm like a dream child. What's worse is that my parents knew I didn't do it. I didn't get grounded for the baby powder. I got grounded for being rude to my principal, the jerk face. Oops.

I laid awake for most of the night, angry at the world. I knew my stupid brother framed me, but I couldn't prove it. All he had done was hand me my backpack. A few dozen kids could've slipped the baby powder into my backpack during class while I wasn't looking.

I woke up the next morning with no earthly purpose. Everything that I held dear had been torn from me. Well, except my PlayStation and subscription to Coding magazine, but everything else, gone. School was my prison and Principal Buthaire was the warden. He had gone too far this time and innocent lives were ruined. Not only was I grounded, but I had in-school suspension, which meant no Sophie in science class. It was time to make a stand.

But how? I moped over to my closet and searched through my shirts. Everything was meh. I jammed my toe on a bin at the bottom of my closet. "Oww!" I yelled as I grabbed my big toe and jumped up and down. I had the misfortune of landing on a dagger of a Lego piece, which nearly sliced my foot off, but surprisingly didn't leave any marks. I stumbled back and tripped over a random sneaker. Both my feet flew out from under me as I fell to the ground flat on my back with a thud and a giant groan.

I lay on the ground for a minute before rolling to my side, angry at the world and the great Lego company. I looked over to see the bin that broke my back was filled with my old Halloween costumes. At the top of the bin was last year's costume, a prison uniform. It had grey and white stripes complete with a prison number and matching cap. My big stand was staring me in the face.

I got dressed quickly and walked out for breakfast dressed as a prisoner. Life as art. Just like dodge ball. Lol.

"Dude, that's awesome. I love it," Derek said, grinning from ear to ear.

That should've been the first warning sign that things were not going to go well for me, but in my funk, I missed it.

I sat in in-school suspension, catching up on my work. It was actually nice not having to listen to the teachers. I'm more of a reader than a listener. With all the quiet, I was able to read a week's worth of history lessons in less than one period.

And then the loudspeaker of evil crackled, which only meant terrible things were coming. It then emitted a muffled, "Sorry to interrupt. Please send Austin Davenport to the principal's office. I repeat, Austin Davenport to the principal's office."

My fellow suspensioners oohed and ahhed, as I stood up.

Adam Borovsky thrust his fist into the air. "Fight the power!"

I responded with a weak fist in the air. I knew what was coming. I didn't know exactly what, but I knew my new nemesis, Principal Buthaire, was up to something. And that was never good.

I entered Principal Buthaire's office. It smelled like baby powder. I was so angry. I hated baby powder and even some babies at that moment. Principal Buthaire was waiting for me. His eye twitched as he studied my outfit from head to toe. "I'm not going to even bother with an explanation because you just don't seem to care about the rules, Mr. Davenport." He ripped a detention slip off his pad and handed it to me. "Detention," he said simply and firmly.

"Detention? For what?"

"For this outfit."

"For wearing stripes and numbers?"

"Uh, yeah." Principal Buthaire's lack of confidence, gave me some of my own.

""Ricky Howell is wearing a soccer jersey with stripes

and a number. I don't see him in your office. Did he get detention?"

"That's none of your concern," he said, snippily.

"What's wrong with my outfit?" I questioned, angrily.

"Watch your tone, mister. It's in clear violation of the code of conduct. Section twelve."

"There is no section twelve."

"There is. It just hasn't been published yet. And as you seem to be very familiar with the code of conduct, section nine succinctly states that changes to the most recent code are valid even if those changes have not been communicated to those subject to it." Principal Buthaire straightened his clip-on tie and smirked.

He was right. It did say that. It wasn't fair, but it was there. "How is that fair? It basically gives you a free pass to punish anyone for anything even when the rule didn't exist at the time. This is...un-American!"

"I've had enough of this. You have detention for a week!" Principal Buthaire tore off detention slips frantically. "Don't do the crime if you can't do the time, Mr. Davenport!"

"I didn't do anything wrong!" I took the detention slips, crumpled them up, and walked back to in-school suspension.

As I settled back into my seat in in-school suspension, the loudspeaker crackled. The students, and even Mr. Braverman, the in-school suspension proctor, groaned.

"This is Principal Buthaire. Unfortunately, I was just forced to give out my five hundredth detention slip this year. This level of unruly behavior is unacceptable! You have forced me to cancel the Halloween dance."

What? My heart sank. My brain flooded with angry thoughts. My liver was on the verge of shutting down. And don't even ask about my appendix. Without Sophie as my date, I was just a nerd. She made me somebody. We were Saustin. I couldn't go back to plain Austin.

The lunatic running our school continued, "You have no one to blame but yourselves and...Austin Davenport. Good day." The loudspeaker clicked off. Before my ears and brain could process what had just been said, all of my major organs burst into volcanic ash and I crashed to the floor, passed out.

11

With a little rest at the nurse's office, a drink of water, and an ice pack for my forehead, all of my organs morphed back into human form. Physically, I was back to normal. Mentally and emotionally? I was a wreck. My thoughts got the better of me. I berated myself for ruining the dance for Sophie, me, and everyone else. I felt sick to my stomach knowing that the whole school hated me. The only person that was probably happy about the dance being canceled was my brother and he hated me, too, for just existing.

The school bell rang. I got up and left the nurse's office. I moped to detention. My life was chock full of excitement. I spent all day in in-school suspension, the nurse's office, and finished it all off in after-school detention. I stared at the ground and tried to blend in as everyone rushed to get their books and catch their buses, but it's kind of hard to blend in when you're wearing a prison outfit in middle school. I got all sorts of stares and stuff thrown at me from erasers to crumpled up pieces of paper. I wanted them all to know that nobody was more disappointed than I was, but I couldn't muster up the words to say any of it. And they probably wouldn't have cared, anyway.

I saw Zorch sweeping on the other side of the hallway. He waved. I just walked by.

Ben ran up to me. "Hey, why aren't you heading to the bus?"

"Detention," I said, barely moving my jaw.

"Oh, forgot. We're going for pizza. Come after."

I had penciled in an exciting afternoon, just wallowing in self-pity. I was too busy for pizza. "I have a pity party to attend."

"Come on, dude. It's pizza!"

It was my favorite. Dough, sauce, cheese, all impeccably arranged and melted together. It was hard to say no. "I could have pizza at my pity party. You'll have to entice me with more than that."

"Just trust me."

"I trust no one, anymore."

"Dude, you're worse than I thought," Ben said, scratching his head.

"I'm the worstest," I mumbled, not sure that was even a word.

"Sammie said she invited Sophie," Ben said.

My ears perked up, but then I realized and said, "She probably hates me."

"She said she was coming. We're getting the dance back."

Energy surged through me like a race car revving its engine. "I'll be there."

When I arrived at Frank's Pizza, the place was hopping. I got frown from Frank and a lot of evil looks from all of the students. I think even some of the old people were mad at me.

"Nice work, Davenport," Ron Boffoli said, his teeth gritted.

I ignored him and all the others and walked past. I saw Ben, Sammie, Luke Hill, Charles "Just Charles" Zaino (call him Charlie, I dare you, and dig your grave if you call him Chuck), Sophie, and a half-eaten pizza pie.

Ben was quick to slide a piece of pizza to the open seat to make sure I stuck around. He didn't realize I was reinvigorated.

Sophie ran up to me and wrapped her arms around me. "Are you okay? I can't believe this happened to you. It's so unfair." I was more than okay. She hugged me! It may have been the best moment of my life up until that point. You may find that sad, but I really liked her.

Sophie grabbed me by my hand and led me to the empty chair. She sat down next to me and smiled.

Ben cleared his throat and banged the parmesan cheese shaker on the table like a judge's gavel. "I call this meeting to order." Ben was much more official than normal. I was glad he was taking this seriously. I just didn't know what we could do. He continued, "The purpose of this meeting is to get the Halloween dance reinstated-"

"And Principal Buthaire fired," Sophie interrupted. My like may have turned to love at that moment.

Everyone nodded in agreement. Just Charles gave her a fist bump.

"But how do we do it?" I asked. "He makes all the rules. And even when it's not a rule, he has a loophole to create them after the fact." I explained the infamous section twelve of the code of conduct. Nobody could believe it.

"Who knew duct tape could ruin all our lives," Sammie said, shaking her head.

Ben chewed on his crust, and with food still in his mouth, asked, "What if we had our own dance?"

"Sounds good, but also sounds expensive," Sophie said.

"Yeah, who's going to pay for it?" Luke asked.

"Good point," Ben whispered, tapping his chin.

"Wait a second. I don't even think the school pays for the dance," I said.

"So how can the school cancel it?" Sammie asked.

"They can't. Or he can't, is more like it," Ben answered.

"Who pays for it then?" Sophie asked.

I smiled. "The PTA. My mother is a chaperone." I looked at Sophie and shrugged. "Sorry about that in advance."

"So what? Sammie asked.

"What's Jimmy Trugman's house phone number?" I asked.

Ben and Luke searched their phones. Luke said, "Got it. What are you going to do with it?"

"His mom's the PTA president." Luke gave me the number. I dialed it. "Hi, Mrs. Trugman. This is Austin Davenport...I'm good. Are you aware that Principal Buthaire canceled the Halloween dance?"

"The heck he did!" Mrs. Trugman screamed through the phone. "I despise that man!" Welcome to the club, Mrs. T. "I hope the board fires him."

"What board?" I asked.

"The school board," she said, simply.

"They can fire him? Tell him what to do?" I asked. I remembered hearing about the school board, but I didn't really care about what they did or didn't do until that moment.

"Yes," Mrs. Trugman said.

"How can I meet with them?" My friends looked at me like I was crazy.

"There is really only one way. They won't meet with you privately or individually. You have to speak at a meeting."

"Speak, like give a presentation?" I asked nervously.

"Maybe a little bit, but it's more like a conversation. In front of everyone."

I felt like my pizza was reversing on me. "Okay. Thank you, Mrs. Trugman."

"Austin, it will take courage to stand up there and stand up against your principal, but it's the right thing to do and you can do it."

"Okay," I said, not convinced. My hand shook as I hung up the phone. I hoped Sophie hadn't noticed.

I stared into a fabulous swirl of melted cheese and sauce, frozen.

Ben shook my shoulder. "Well?" he said.

"Well, what?" I asked.

"Are you gonna do it?"

∾

"Speak in front of the board?" I asked, but continued without waiting for an answer, "I have to." And then I hurled my pizza into Sophie's lap. Just kidding, but it did seem like a strong possibility at the time.

The night of the school board meeting was here. I barely

ate dinner. My stomach was in knots. As my mother drove the two of us to the meeting, I stared out the window, trying to forget what I was about to do. We got there early. I wanted to be first on the speaking list and sit near the front. If nothing else, I just wanted to be done with it. I signed up and my mom and I sat in the second row. I turned around as everyone was still filing in. I kept looking for my friends, but no one was there yet. I wasn't sure if I even wanted them there. There was a good chance I would freeze up there and look like an idiot.

The excitement died down once the meeting started. Because, well, adult meetings are boring. There's a reason why kids don't usually attend. They started with the Pledge of Allegiance and then it was a snore fest from there.

I passed the time reading over my speech, hoping that it would calm my nerves. It didn't. After a whole bunch of really boring stuff, it was time for audience comments. The board president, a portly man with a clean-shaven head, leaned into the microphone on the table in front of him and said, "We will take questions and comments from the public before closing with an ad-hoc budget request. Mr. Austin Davenport, please step up to the mic."

I had no idea what an ad-hoc budget request was, but it was time. I wasn't sure if it was go time or throw up time, but it was my time. I stood up, my knees shaking. My mom rubbed my elbow and smiled at me. I forced a smile and walked into the aisle. I stepped up to the podium and adjusted the microphone. I took a deep breath and thought about running for the emergency exit.

None of my friends bothered to show up to support me. And then something crazy happened. Numerous doors opened across the back of the auditorium and people started filing in. Like a lot of them. I saw Ben, Luke, Sammie,

Sophie, Just Charles, and just about every other kid I knew from school walk in with their parents. Some sat down in the many open seats. Others just stood in the back, lining the wall. There must have been a hundred people, maybe more.

It was insane. I looked at my friends and they all gave me a thumbs up. I looked around and couldn't let everyone down. I saw Principal Buthaire and almost changed my mind. He looked at me as if I had just puked on his shoes. I could only imagine how angry and disgusted he would be after I blasted him. Not to mention how many detention slips I would get afterwards.

I took a deep breath and cleared my throat. I looked at the seven board members. "Ladies and gentlemen," I said as confidently as I could. "As you might have heard, the Halloween dance was canceled by Principal Buthaire." I could feel his eyes staring at me, but I refused to look at him. Otherwise, I thought I would lose my nerve. If I lost, I ran the risk of an even rockier relationship with him. And if I won, it could be that much worse. I was risking a lot, but the potential reward of a dance date with Sophie was worth it.

I continued, "He blamed our misbehavior, specifically mine. This happened just after I received a week's detention for wearing a prison costume to school in protest of the principal's overbearing rules. I did not violate the dress code by wearing stripes and a number. It is no different than a soccer jersey. No tank top, no inappropriate words, phrases, or graphics. My pants were worn at the waist. I wore Nike sneakers." I paused as I looked at my mom for reassurance. She smiled and nodded. My confidence rose a little. I added a, "Furthermore," pointing my finger to the ceiling for effect, and continued, "Even if I did violate the dress code, canceling the dance was not an appropriate response."

I looked across at the board members and they were all listening intently. I almost felt bad for how boring I found it when they were talking, but I had bigger things to worry about. I continued, "The Halloween dance is a PTA-sponsored event, paid for by dues from parents and fundraisers from children and parents. It is not a school budget decision. Principal Buthaire has no right to cancel it for any reason. I asked Mrs. Trugman, the PTA president, to attend this meeting to answer any questions you might have about this."

Mrs. Trugman smiled and waved to the board. I ended my speech with, "Thank you for your time. I hope you will restore the Halloween dance and our faith in humanity." I thought that last bit might've been a little bit too much, but based on the standing ovation that burst out after I was done, I guess it was okay.

My friends were jumping up and down, cheering and screaming my name. I think I may have even heard someone yell, "It's time to shave the butt hair!" I looked at my mom and Mrs. Trugman and they were beaming. Principal Buthaire? Not so much. His face was so purple, he looked like he morphed into a very unhappy eggplant.

"Thank you, Mr. Davenport. You may be seated," the

bald man said calmly. He then looked at Mrs. Trugman. "Can you confirm that Mr. Davenport's complaint is 100% accurate?"

I wasn't sure how she would answer that question, based on my comment about restoring faith in humanity, but she said, "Yes. I can. Austin is correct. The PTA funds the entire dance. It is the PTA's stance that the dance should take place as originally planned."

"Thank you. First off, I congratulate you, Mr. Davenport, for standing up here tonight. It is never easy, particularly when you have an issue with a teacher or a principal." People clapped. I nodded, my heart racing while we waited for the verdict. "To the matter at hand, I put to our board, all in favor of reinstating the Cherry Avenue Halloween dance?"

The other six board members all answered in unison, "Aye." I assumed that was good, because my mom hugged me and most of the auditorium burst out into applause. I smiled at my mom and shook the hand of the guy in front of me.

The president interrupted the cheers, "Quiet down, please. We still have one matter to attend to." The cheers died down and the bald man continued, "The board received an ad-hoc budget request last week from the administration. In it, twenty thousand dollars was requested for video cameras, software, and service as an ongoing safety initiative. All in favor?"

The remaining board members said, "Aye."

The president then said, "Those against?" The rest of the board remained silent.

The president smiled. "The budget request is approved. We appreciate the administration's effort to stay on top of the security of our children."

I finally had the guts to look over at Principal Buthaire and he was smiling, twisting his sinister mustache. Uh, oh. What did I miss? Had my crushing defeat of his plan melted his brain?

"And that concludes our meeting," the president said with a smile. "Good night."

It took us over an hour to get home. I received so many congratulatory handshakes from kids and parents, and even a few board members. While my Mom was busy receiving congratulations from various parents, Principal Buthaire whispered in my ear, "You may have won the battle, but I just won the war. And by the way, while you were speaking, your fly was open."

My mouth dropped open, not just because I couldn't believe what he said about the war, but I reached for my zipper and realized it was, in fact, open. Ahhhhh, farts.

12

I got off the bus the next morning to high-fives, chest bumps, and one autograph request. The only person besides Principal Buthaire angry about the dance being back on was my brother. He pushed his way through the crowd gathering around me, muttering to himself. I didn't really care. He could use a few lessons in losing.

Winning. It was awesome. It didn't happen often, so I was enjoying it. Kids I didn't even know were congratulating me on the way to Advisory. Even girls. That's huge for a kid like me. Seventh and eighth graders, too.

As I stuffed my backpack into my locker, a seventh grader, Zoey Hicks, slid up next to me. "Hey Austin," she said with a smile.

"Umm, hi." She surprised me. Not only by sneaking up on me, but she was a cute seventh grader and normally wouldn't be caught dead talking to me. I felt like it was Opposite Day.

"It was so impressive how you stood up to the principal. Not everyone could do that," she said as she leaned in close.

She was a close talker. Ugh. I hated those. And while she was cute, her breath wasn't. Do people eat tuna fish for breakfast?

"Thanks. I just didn't think it was fair," I said.

"It wasn't."

We just looked at each other for a few seconds, neither of us seemingly knowing what to say. "Soooo," I managed to whisper.

"So," she said and then looked behind me and then back at me. "Okay. See you later." She turned on her heels and walked away.

"Umm, bye." Weirdo. I shrugged my shoulders and headed to class.

The next few periods were pretty cool. Lots of kids were paying attention to me. Even a few teachers took me aside to tell me they were proud of me. And then it all ended in the blink of an eye.

As I walked to class, I turned a corner and my mouth dropped open. I saw the new security cameras being installed. Inside! I thought they were for outside the buildings. It was then that I knew why Principal Buthaire was so excited when the board approved them. It was his death blow to all of us. It was him winning the war.

Ben sprinted up to me, shouting, "We have a problem!"

"I know!" I pointed to the cameras.

"That's not what I was talking about."

I hung my head. "What now?" I said to the floor.

Ben screeched to a halt in front of me. "Well, you have a problem. I'm in pretty good shape. Being your best friend is finally paying off for me."

"Hey!" I yelled. "I have feelings, you know!"

"Sorry."

"What's the problem?" I asked. Before Ben could answer, I saw someone resembling Sophie storming down the hallway like the Hulk, swatting people out of her way, her eyes shooting livid lasers into mine. Gulp.

13

Sophie continued her storming down the hallway and added yelling, too. "How could you? I thought you were one of the nice ones! But I guess now that you're a celebrity…"

"How could I what?" I looked at Ben. He was no help. He froze like a statue.

"The least you could've done was tell me how you felt about her and broke up with me first!"

"Who?"

"You know who. Don't act dumb."

"I am dumb."

"No you're not!" Sophie yelled. Tears were welling up in her eyes. Not good.

"About this, I am. I have no idea what you're talking about."

"Whatever, we're done. I thought you were different."

"I am." I shrugged. I really didn't know what the heck was going on.

"I don't want to go to the dance with you. And don't want

to be your girlfriend." She rushed away as tears started streaming down her cheeks.

I thought I might cry, too. I stood there in the middle of the hallway, joining Ben in statue form. I whispered to myself, "What just happened?"

"She dumped you," Ben managed to say.

"She was my girlfriend?"

"You are dumb."

"I know that. Why did it happen?"

"Don't get mad at me. You asked the question. Turns out, you've been a victim of social media yet again."

That shook me out of my stupor. I turned to Ben. "Really?" I asked, annoyed. "Now what? Did my brother take a picture of me pooping again?"

"No, but that was a good one," Ben laughed, but quickly turned serious, as he looked at my less-than-amused face. "Sorry, not helping. There's a picture of you circulating with Zoey Hicks and it says that you are dating. It looks like you're kissing."

"Really?" My heart dropped. The whole thing did seem weird at the time.

Some dude walked by holding his phone up to show me. "Nice one, dude," he said, unhelpfully. I took a close look and it did look like Zoey was kissing me. Underneath it, a caption read, 'Our new hero has a new girlfriend!' My stomach was in knots.

"I think I was set up."

"Derek," Ben said. It was all he had to say. We both knew it.

And what's worse, I heard a whirring sound coming from the corner above me. I looked up to see a security camera turning toward me. It came to a stop as I came into its path. Principal Buthaire was watching.

14

Despite my stand against the prison-like conditions of Cherry Avenue Middle School, the arrival of the security cameras made things infinitely worse. Principal Buthaire watched our every move. B.C. (Before Cameras), you only got in trouble if you were physically caught saying or doing something wrong, unless you got framed with baby powder and ratted out, of course. A.C. (After Cameras), Principal Buthaire had our Advisory teachers hand out detention slips for the previous school day's infractions. It was like the lottery. But instead of winning millions of dollars, you got detention. Lucky us. Morale. Was. Low. And rightly so.

School was a dreary disaster. The kids turned into robots as soon as the bus door opened- heads down, no talking, straight to class. And detention participation increased so dramatically that it had to be move to the cafeteria.

The days all blended together like one big zombie fest. I can't remember most of October. I was still serving out my detentions every day for getting framed for the baby powder incident. I was one of the few seemingly perpetual attendees. Principal Buthaire limited his vendetta to one lucky student: me. I guess that was good for everyone else, but for me, not so much. And Sophie wanted nothing to do with me. I couldn't convince her that nothing happened with Zoey.

So I decided to do something about it. Zoey Hicks and I crossed paths every day on my way to Spanish. I was going to confront her. She normally ignored me, looked back over her shoulder as I was passing, tied her shoe, whatever she could to avoid looking at me. As I turned the corner and entered the foreign language wing, our version of the countries at Epcot, I spotted Zoey immediately, walking down the hallway with Nick DeRozan, a hulking football player. Ugh. I wasn't happy about it, but it wasn't going to stop me.

As I approached Zoey, she pulled one of the signature moves I typically get when girls see me. She turned to her right, away from me, and waved, pretending to say hi to a friend. There was not a single person there. I cut over and stopped right in front of her.

"Hi, Zoey!" I said, enthusiastically.

"Hey, umm, you."

I tried not to look at Nick, whose nasal breathing resembled that of a bull and blew my hair around like a tornado.

I looked into Zoey's eyes. "Why did you do that to me? It ruined my life."

"I don't know what you're talking about," she whispered as she looked down at the ground.

"Let's go," a deep voice boomed from above me. Was it Nick DeRozan or God speaking to me from the heavens? I wasn't sure. But then Nick grabbed Zoey's arm and walked her around me. I turned and watched as they walked away. Zoey turned to look at me and then quickly turned away. That didn't go as I had hoped. I wanted a full confession, complete with an apology letter to Sophie. All I got was a recurring nightmare about a bull named Nick that wanted to run me over.

My life was basically back to normal. Everyone had pretty much forgotten I lost them the dance and then got the dance back. I guess I didn't blame them. They kind of evened each other out. I was nearing one of my final days of detention.

As I walked into the cafeteria, Dr. Dinkledorf was waiting for me. "Mr. Davenport, a word?"

I nodded. What now? Was I getting summoned to the principal's office for more detention for using too much glue in art? Or suspended for not eating enough veggies during lunch? Or maybe expelled for thinking? "What is it, sir?" I asked, concerned.

"'If a law is unjust, a man is not only right to disobey it, he is obligated to do so.' Thomas Jefferson said that." He searched my eyes for signs of life.

"I don't know what to do," I admitted.

"I can't tell you what to do, but perhaps you could skip ahead in our history books since you are such a great student. I suggest reading about such topics as civil disobedience, the Boston Tea Party, boycotts, and walkouts. Solely for your education, of course."

"Of course," I said. He wanted me to start an uprising. And I had nothing to lose in doing so. Well, besides getting kicked out of school. At that point, I was okay with that.

Later that night, just after dinner, I was alone in my bedroom, or war room, which was a better description of it at the time. I had charts, maps, and a whole host of lists scattered about. I had reassembled our team from Frank's Pizza. Well, all except for one. I'm guessing you know which one that was. I stared at my phone, wanting to text Sophie, but afraid it would end in the one thousandth case of rejection I had received from her since the whole Zoey Hicks horror show. It still stung every time. Even number 999. I wasn't too keen on another slap in the face.

I didn't want to give up, though. She was too special. And I didn't do anything wrong! It just wasn't right. And I needed to right this wrong before I righted any other wrongs. I texted her, 'Can we please talk?' along with a gif of a cat with big eyes, begging. She liked cats, but hated me. I wasn't sure which one would win. I waited a few minutes. Nothing. I tried not to let it bother me, but it did. I texted her again. And again. And again. Nothing but a whole chain of unanswered texts.

I thought about abandoning the effort and focusing on taking down Buthaire, but I couldn't stop thinking about Sophie. I stared at my phone for what seemed like an hour, hoping she would, willing her to text me back. Even if it was just to tell me to leave her alone. Being ignored was much worse. Finally, the text app showed a bubble pop up, indicating she was typing on the other end. My heart leapt. And then crashed when the bubble disappeared into thin air. Ugh.

So I decided to call her. I took a deep breath and pushed the button. I would've been less nervous launching a nuclear weapon. The phone rang. My pulse jumped higher with each ring. After five rings, I heard a click. I waited for her voice to say hello, but it was a computerized voice from her voice mail. I hung up, dejected. I called again ten minutes later. Still no answer. I decided to leave a message. After the beep, I said, "Sophie, this is Austin. Please don't hang up. I swear to you on my PlayStation, Pokémon collection, my parents, my science camp, all the most important things in my life that she did not kiss me. I was framed. I swear to you. Please. Please. Please. Call me back. Please."

I tried to shift my focus to planning the Buthaire takedown, but I got nowhere. I came to the conclusion that since Sophie didn't call me back, I probably hadn't said, 'please,' enough, so I called her back again. The phone rang and I heard a click and then Sophie's voice! "Hello," she said, "this is Sophie. Please leave a message." My heart dropped. I thought she had actually answered. And then I wondered why she changed her message until I heard the rest of it, "Unless you are Austin Davenport and then your call will not be returned." I dropped the phone. My jaw hit the bed first. I couldn't believe it.

Then my phone dinged. A text! I closed my mouth and reached for the phone so frantically that I almost threw it halfway across the room. When I finally had control of it, I looked to see who it was from. I begged and pleaded that it I was from Sophie. Unfortunately, it was not. It was from Ben. I feel bad saying it, but I was disappointed. And then disgusted.

The text read, 'Derek asked Sophie to the dance!' I

nearly threw up. I clicked on the message because there was more. I exhaled when the rest said, 'and she said no!'. It would've been a Kung-Fu kick to my soul if she had said yes. But still, she wasn't going with me, either, so nothing really had changed for the better.

But how could I change that? She wasn't taking my calls. She ignored me in class. She avoided me in the hallways. And then it came to me. I was going to her house and wasn't going to leave until she forgave me. Or called the police.

15

I rushed to my closet and grabbed my camping backpack. I was going to be prepared. I didn't know how long it would take. Hours, days, weeks even...I walked out of my room, brushing shoulders with Derek on my way down the hall.

"Where are you going?" I ignored him and kept focused on my mission.

In the kitchen, I packed my bag with as many snacks and bottles of water it could fit. I rifled through some camping gear in the garage and a rain poncho. I had one more item to secure and it proved my determination. I went to the bathroom to put on one of my great-aunt Catherine's diapers that we had left over from when she visited a while back. Yep, I was all in.

It was squishy, but manageable. I tried to look cool as I walked out of the bathroom and toward the front door. My mother and sister were sitting in the living room just off the foyer. I strapped on my pack, and then grabbed the desk chair from the computer. Everyone looked at me, quizzically.

My mother finally had the courage to ask, "Where are you going with all that?"

I said simply, "To win Sophie back." And then walked out the door, a man on a mission.

I arrived at 12 Oak Street at about 8:00, pushing all of my stuff on the rolling chair. It was definitely getting darker, but it wasn't pitch black just yet, plus dozens of street lights ran up and down the sidewalks. I threw my backpack to the ground and plopped into my chair, not sure what else to do. I sat there for about twenty minutes, hoping someone in Sophie's house would notice me, but it looked dark inside.

The only attention I got was from a grade-school kid on a bike. He rolled to a stop and looked at me. "What're you doing?"

I looked at him as confidently as I could and said, "Winning. Thanks for stopping by."

He looked at me like I was a little crazy, which I can't blame him for. I was a little crazy. Or a lot.

I waited for at least another twenty minutes before seeing any other action and then I heard a car approach from behind me. A black SUV rolled up the driveway. Sophie's father stepped out of the SUV and did a double take. He looked at me sideways.

"Hello, Sir. Wonderful night, isn't it?" I asked, trying to make my presence there as normal as possible.

The man frowned. "I thought so, until now. Is there a reason you're camped out there, guy?"

"Yes." The less info I gave the better. I looked away, hoping his questions would stop.

He still had more. "Care to share it?"

"Not really."

"Okay," he said. "You look familiar." He shrugged and walked toward the front door. He pushed the door open. I heard him say, "Anyone know the weird kid sitting out in front of the house?"

Sophie, a little boy, and Sophie's mom looked out the front window.

I heard Sophie say, "I do." She was less than enthusiastic.

Sophie emerged from the house and walked down the driveway toward me. She looked slightly less mad than when she Hulked out about Zoey Hicks.

"I thought I told you it was over," she spat.

"You did." I nodded, not sure what else to say.

"So why are you here?"

"To win you back."

"But it's over."

"That was based on a false premise."

She huffed and looked up at the sky, perhaps praying I would disappear. "You can't just stay here."

"Why not?"

"This is our property."

"That is incorrect. It is the town's property, but unfortunately you are required to maintain its upkeep. It's very unfair, I know. Kind of like dumping someone based on a rumor that you don't bother to confirm or discuss with said dumpee, for example, me."

"I saw the picture!" she yelled.

"It's not real."

She huffed and walked away. Over her shoulder, she called out, "Stay here all night for all I care. I don't have to talk to you."

"I will. There's nothing that's going to keep me from staying."

Sophie stormed into the house and slammed the door behind her. I took a deep breath and reached into my bag for a drink. As I cracked open a water bottle, I heard a strange hissing sound. I didn't know where it was coming from until it was too late. A sprinkler blasted me in the ear. I felt like I was back at the car wash. At least nobody saw this one happen. And then I heard a car door shut. I wiped the water out of my face and moved my chair out of the way of the sprinkler, which was headed back my way.

I looked over at the car and saw my dad walking toward me. I frowned and shook my head.

"Your mother told me about your little stakeout here," my father said, as he put his arm around me. "I know you like her, but there are probably better ways to get her back than stalking her on her front lawn."

"This isn't stalking. This is public property. I have a right to be here!" The pitch of my voice rose higher and higher with each word.

"Okay. Okay. I can see you believe very strongly about this."

"I do. I'm staying."

"I hear you loud and clear. If you're staying, I'm staying."

"Why?"

"Because I can't let my kid sleep in the street alone."

"Can you at least stay in the car?"

"Okay, bud." My dad stood up and folded up his chair. "Let me know if you need anything."

"You let *me* know. I brought just about everything."

My dad smiled and patted me on the shoulder, laughing. "Will do."

I took out my phone (fully charged, of course) and took a selfie, smiling. I posted it on Snapchat with the words, 'I will stay outside Sophie's house until proven innocent.' I should've still been wearing my prisoner costume.

And then I got the break I had been waiting for. My phone buzzed with a text. It was from Luke. It was a screenshot from Snapchat. It was from Zoey Hicks. It said, 'It wuz setup...No kiss. Never going out. It wuz cruel joke. Sorry to Auggie.'

My name was Austin, but Auggie was good enough, maybe even better. It just showed there was nothing between us. I threw my phone down on the grass and celebrated like I scored the game-winning touchdown. I flossed like a boss. I immediately sent the message to Sophie. I waited for the lights to go on inside the house and for her to rush into my arms, begging for my forgiveness, but nothing happened. I kept checking my phone to see if I missed her response, but there was nothing. Eventually, I grabbed a light blanket out of my backpack and fell asleep.

A tap on my shoulder startled me awake. I opened my eyes to see Sophie leaning over me. I was shocked at first, not understanding why she was in my bedroom waking me up, but then I remembered my camp out. I quickly wiped the slobber from my chin. I'm not a pretty sleeper. I hoped she hadn't heard me snoring.

"Good morning," she said, and smiled.

I looked at her confused. "Am I still dreaming?"

She laughed. "No. I'm sorry for not believing you. Please forgive me." She inhaled a deep breath and looked like she was about to begin a long-winded speech. I shushed her and grabbed her lips with two fingers and closed them. It was not as smooth as I envisioned.

"You had me at 'good morning'," I said.

She laughed and shook her head.

I continued, "It's all forgiven. Never happened. As long as you're going to the dance with me." I crossed my fingers on both hands and put on my best smile.

"Yes. If you still want to go with me. I was a jerk."

"A little," I said through a smile. "But I definitely still want to go with you. And I really want to get out of this diaper." I stood up and looked down at my diaper-filled pants.

"You're wearing a diaper?" Sophie's eyes bulged.

"Yes. Please don't tell anyone."

"I have to. It's the sweetest thing anyone's ever done for me."

"Please?"

"Okay, but you have to tell me if you used it."

"That's none of your concern."

She gave me a puppy-dog look.

I sighed. "I peed once."

Sophie cracked up. Had I done #2, I would've called the whole thing off.

"Can we have breakfast together?"

"Only if you're wearing a wet diaper, too," I said.

"Okay, rain check then."

"Or I could meet you for lunch?" I asked.

"I would love that."

Me, too.

16

I walked into the house, all smiles. My dad followed behind me. I threw my oversized backpack on the foyer floor and ran up to change my diaper and shower. It was one of the best showers of my life. Now I know why babies cry so much when they're wet. Diapers are disgusting. Anyway, let's never talk about this again.

I went downstairs into the kitchen. My whole family was sitting at the table having breakfast.

My mother looked at me and said, "Well? Your father won't tell us what happened."

A smile broke out across my face. I wanted to do a dance and tell Derek I won and he lost, but I kept it together and said, "It worked! We're going to the dance together."

"Oh, that's great, honey!" my mother said.

"Nice work, lover boy," Leighton said through a smile.

I looked at Derek who was staring at his cereal like Raisin Bran was the most interesting thing he had ever seen.

Leighton couldn't help herself. "Hey Derek, isn't that the girl you wanted to take to the dance?"

I could see him bite his lip. He whisper mumbled, "Yes."

"What's that? I couldn't hear you?"

"Leighton, knock it off," my dad said with a stern look.

I tried to hold in a smile, but didn't do a great job. Leighton winked at me.

"Grab a bowl, you two," my mother said.

Derek never told me for certain, but I know that it was at that moment that he vowed to bring down the Halloween Dance. I noticed a look on his face, one that could not be trusted. I didn't know what he was going to do until the next day.

I figured it out when I was deep undercover in a special ops mission: Operation Big Brother Takedown. I had two big brother problems. One, my real big brother, and two, the man, big brother, watching us on camera. I vowed to take down the security system. But it was going to be difficult. Rules would be broken. Austin could be grounded and expelled. Yes, I'm referring to myself in the third person. It's fair game when you're talking about yourself during special missions. I would tell you my code name, but you don't have the security clearance. Sorry.

I sat near the window during English class. It was the one time I was grateful that the school didn't have air conditioning. The windows were open, which would make my escape much easier. I chose English for two specific purposes: it was close to Principal Buthaire's office window, who had lunch at that time, and as I mentioned earlier, Mrs. Conklin doesn't stop her lesson plans even if kids start jumping out of the first floor window.

Mrs. Conklin turned around to write something on the board and I knew it was time. I gave Ronnie Winslow a nod. I handed him my notebook and slinked over to the window. I climbed up and out the window, landing on my feet like a cat. It was only two feet from the ground, but I'm not the most coordinated kid, so I was proud that I didn't fall on my face. My confidence was perhaps a little too high, though. As I approached the windows of the next classroom on my way to The Butt Crack (my new name for Principal Buthaire's office), I took it up a notch and yelled, "Dive roll!" as I dive rolled under the window. I then realized that when attempting a stealth maneuver like the dive roll, you shouldn't call out the move. It tends to make you unstealthy. I had to shush a few kids that had rushed to the windows in the courtyard. They saw I was headed to The Butt Crack and immediately let me be.

I approached the opening of The Butt Crack and looked around the courtyard to make sure no one was watching. All clear. I peeked into The Butt Crack to make sure there was no Buthaire. It was all clear. I took a deep breath and then climbed up into The Crack. As soon as my feet hit the floor, I slid into Principal Buthaire's chair.

My mission was to crash the security camera system, but I had to take a detour once I saw the picture of Principal and Mrs. Buthaire staring at me next to the computer monitor. I whispered to myself, "I shouldn't." But I did. I grabbed a black marker from the principal's pen holder that said, '#1 Principal'. I guess they sold those things to anyone. I couldn't help myself. I drew a curly mustache on Mrs. Buthaire and devil horns on Principal Buthaire. This was war.

I swear I've always been a good kid, listened to my teach-ers, respected my principal, but this guy was the worst. I laughed to myself as I admired my artwork. I then moved onto the mission. I shook the computer mouse and woke up the computer. I scanned the desktop icons and found a folder named, 'security'. Each camera had its own folder of saved footage. I deleted each of them one by one. When I got to the camera outside my Spanish class, I whispered, "Borra," which means 'erase' in Spanish. Señora Fuentes would be proud. At least of my Spanish vocabulary knowl-edge. When I got to the east wing bathroom files, I wondered if Principal Buthaire knew about Max Mulvihill. I erased that one and then the entire program that ran the cameras.

I smiled, proud of my work. I should've hopped out the window and headed back to class, mission complete, but I was feeling ambitious. I opened Chrome and typed in, 'fart sounds'. I downloaded the first one that popped up and then used it to change the sound of the alert when Principal Buthaire received an email. He was going to love that. I chuckled to myself and then my face dropped as I heard Principal Buthaire outside The Butt Crack.

I hopped up as the door opened, but tripped on the

chair. I fell to the floor, face first. My only move was to hide under the desk. I scrambled underneath it, but I knew I was toast. My heart pounded. I couldn't believe I drew a mustache on his wife! I was so getting expelled. My parents would be furious. I scrunched myself up as much as I could, but if he sat down and rolled toward the desk, there was no hiding.

I heard the door close and then footsteps. Principal Buthaire's voice surprised me, "Mr. Davenport." How did he find me? I almost answered and came out, but something told me to keep my mouth shut.

"Yes, sir?" Derek responded. I was shocked. What was he doing there?

I searched for my phone to text Ben for a distraction, but I left it in my locker. I was stuck. I thought about just making a run for it and jumping out the window, but it was too risky.

"How did you feel about the Halloween dance being canceled?"

"I was happy."

"Good. I need you to right a wrong," Principal Buthaire said. "Can I trust you to keep a secret?"

"Yes. What do you need me to do?" Derek asked, curiously.

"I need you to make sure that the Halloween dance doesn't happen. Can you do that?"

Derek didn't answer for a minute. "If you promise I won't get in trouble."

"I do. You'll be my hero. You can make your own schedule, get a few extra lockers-"

"Can I change my grades?"

"No."

"Hang out in the teacher's lounge?"

"Why would you want to do that?"

"I don't know. Because none of the other kids can."

"No, but I will look the other way on all of the detentions I've been handing out. Do we have a deal?"

"Yes," Derek said.

I was seething. I wanted to jump out and yell, "Gotcha!", but I kinda wasn't supposed to be there.

"Alright. Back to class. And don't tell anyone about this."

"Yes, sir."

The door closed. Principal Buthaire walked over to his desk. My heart rate surged higher with each foot step. I was staring at his shoes. He put his hand on his chair, spun it around, and then something glorious happened. The fire alarm rang. Principal Buthaire huffed. "Now what?" he mumbled.

I watched as his shoes disappeared. I exhaled and wiped the sweat from my forehead. I was saved. And then it happened. The computer farted. I swear it wasn't me.

"What the?" Principal Buthaire said. I heard him sniffing the air. And then the computer farted again. Principal Buthaire sniffed his way all the way to the window. My heart rate was back up at implosion levels. And then the door creaked open.

"Principal Buthaire," a woman's voice said, "We need to leave."

"Yes. Yes, indeed," he said as he walked away from the window and out the door.

Once I heard the door click, I scooted out from underneath the desk and hopped out the window. I saw a crowd filing out of the school a few hundred feet away. I ran as fast as I could and pushed my way into the procession.

❧

I SAT at lunch with Ben. I told them all about the devil's pact that Principal Buthaire and Derek made. I recounted the farting computer and nearly getting caught under Principal Buthaire's desk after breaking into The Butt Crack and erasing all of the security footage.

"I was lucky to escape," I told him.

"There's no such thing as luck." Ben smiled at me.

"You pulled it, Ben?"

"Maybe. Maybe not."

"We're best friends. Really?"

"Okay," he said, giddy. He lowered his voice and continued, "I knew when you were going. It was perfect. Your English class connected to his office through the courtyard and it was when he had lunch."

"Yeah, I know. We planned it that way," I said, getting annoyed.

"Well, what we didn't plan was for Principal Buthaire to leave the teacher's lounge early. I saw him pass by with your brother and I knew there would be trouble."

"Great work," I said, grateful.

"I'll see if Jim Easton can whip up an algorithm to send a

million emails to Buthaire. We can pummel him with fart mail."

And that's why we were best friends.

"Dude, we are like Batman and Robin," I said, laughing.

"I know you think you're Batman, but I'm Batman," Ben said.

"We're both Batman."

"Not possible," he said.

"Your name is Ben Gordon. That's literally the name of the police commissioner. You can't be Batman."

"Whatever," Ben said, annoyed.

"Okay, let's forget it. We still have work to do. We have to stop Derek."

"Right. First off, we need to know your brother's every move before he makes it," Ben said before taking a bite of his turkey sandwich. He dropped it on the tray with disgust. "Do they intentionally suck all of the goodness out of the food here?"

I ignored his complaint. "How are we going to do that? Spy on him?" I smiled after I said it. That was exactly what we were going to do.

"I still have that recording device from a spy kit my grandma gave me. Well, my father took it away because I was listening to all of their conversations, but I'm sure I could get it back."

"How does it work?" I asked, intrigued.

"It's voice activated. Ten hour battery life. Tiny."

"I could put one in the vent by his bedroom. Sometimes, I can hear him on FaceTime through it. But how do we see his texts or conversations in school?"

"You're going to have to hack his phone and read his texts."

I thought for a moment. It was going to be hard. And

then I realized that it would be simple. My dad got all of our texts on some sort of parent spying app. If I could get him to let me use his iPad, I could get easy access to Derek's texts. And then it got even simpler. If my dad read our texts, it likely meant that Derek never texted any of his trouble making.

"I don't think he will text or Snap anything because my dad sees all that stuff," I said. "Get me the bug and I'll do the rest."

In all my years of school, I had never done my homework so quickly and poorly. My entire mission for the evening was to place the bug that Ben had given me somewhere that would pick up all of Derek's bedroom conversations. Check. I opened up the air conditioning vent in my room with the small screwdriver on my pocket knife. I tied a long piece of string around the tiny listening device and chucked it down the vent when Derek went to the bathroom. It clinked and clanked down the vent to a stop. I laid the string down and closed the vent.

I put on the headphones that would transmit those conversations and plopped onto my bed. Now all I had to do was wait for my brother to move his butt chin up and down and blab all of his little secrets. I waited and waited for what seemed like two hours, but nothing. Well, he farted a few times, but that wasn't part of his devious plan. Just a symptom of mom's cauliflower casserole, but it jolted me awake every time I started to doze off and I couldn't smell them through the vent, so I didn't complain.

Another fart rattled my brain through the headphones. I thought my brain might explode.

I sat up, my heart racing, but it quickly faded into disappointment. And then I heard his voice, "Yo, Jay, you'll never guess what happened to me today. Butt Hair asked me to take down the Halloween dance...Yeah, I know. I was gonna do that anyway. And he thinks I'm doing him a favor. This is gonna be awesome...I dunno. There was a rumor going around earlier in the year that I was gonna flood the gym. Maybe I'll do that. My brother doesn't think I could pull it off. This way, I'll ruin the dance and prove him wrong. Win, win, both for me."

Not so fast, bro. We'll just see about that. I couldn't wait to get to school the next day to tell my friends and thwart his thwarting. If that's even a thing. If it's not, it should be.

17

I stood with Ben and Sammie at the bus stop while my brother played football, as always. It was getting cooler and a little bit windy, so it was a good excuse to huddle close. Nobody really cared what we had to say anyway, but we couldn't take any chances. I leaned in and said, "He's going to flood the dance."

"What?" Sammie said entirely too loud. "No way."

I rolled my eyes. "Yes, way. I'll play the voice recording for you later if you want. He told Jayden."

Sammie looked like she was going to cry.

Ben's eyes bulged out of his head. "What are we going to do? That's serious. We should tell your parents."

I pursed my lips. "No. He doesn't know that we know, so we can save the day." I immediately remembered Zorch's ungodly amount of soap in his lair.

I guess I had some sort of smirk on my face, because Ben said, "What? Tell us already. I know you've got something."

I smiled and said, "Yes, I do, friends. What do water and soap equal?"

Sammie looked at me confused, "Soapy water?"

I huffed. "Well, yes, but I meant bubbles."

"Not following, dude," Ben said.

"We can turn the flood into a giant foam party."

"Oh, I like it. I like it muy mucho," Ben said, smiling.

Sammie didn't look as enthusiastic. I knew what she was thinking. "Don't worry, this will keep Derek from getting in trouble. The foam won't cause any damage." She was on board. "Can we meet at your house to design the machine?" I looked at Ben.

"Is a frog's butt watertight?" Ben asked.

"I guess so?" I shrugged.

"It is," Ben said, definitively.

I had no interest in Googling that, so I just took his word for it and showed up at his house after dinner.

We did, however, Google a whole bunch of DIY articles and watch a lot of YouTube. We came across some great ideas until something kind of important came to mind. Ben and I both lay on our stomachs on his bed, his laptop open in front of us.

"Umm," I said, "Teeny, tiny problem."

"What's that?" Ben asked, as he scrolled down a Google search page.

"If my brother floods the gym, not only will the electric short out, including our machine, but people could get hurt. Or worse." And by worse, I meant get dead. I view staying undead as a high priority. Well, not undead like a zombie, but you know what I mean. I think.

"So we need to cut the power and use a battery pack," Ben said, thinking aloud.

"Ok. Assuming we can figure out how to do that and do it without getting in trouble, what then? Are we just gonna stand around in a pile of foam?"

"It's a good thing we're still brainstorming. We probably need some music."

I thought for a moment. "No electric, but we need music. We can bring a Bluetooth speaker. I have one we use for the pool. It's waterproof and everything."

"Will it be loud enough?" Ben asked.

"Not for the whole gym." I slid off the bed and paced around the room. Pacing is necessary for better ideas. "We'll have to break into the main office."

"I see where you're going with this. I like it," Ben said. "Well, that's assuming we don't get expelled. Cutting the power, breaking into the office-"

"Hijacking the sound system," I added.

It was a good thing we were nerds and had access to our Dads' garages because Ben and I had all of the necessary parts to build the foam machine. Don't try this at home, kids! Now cue the music! Here comes the montage! We used a giant paint pail to hold the soap, an old fan as the blower, tweaked a paint pallet to deliver the soap, and a boatload of batteries from all of my remote-controlled cars and trucks. We modified the designs we found on the Internet so that the machine would capture the flooding water.

We stood inside Ben's garage, staring at the finished product as it sat atop a red wagon. "Well, that looks good," I said.

Ben took a deep breath. "I'm nervous, but I think we should test it. Are we going to blow ourselves up?"

"With my luck?" I laughed. Ben didn't join me. "Don't worry, it'll be fine."

I walked out of the garage and around to the side of the house. I filled up a pail of water with the hose as Ben pulled the machine behind me.

"Soap good? We ready?" I asked.

Ben nodded and shrugged. His confidence was inspiring. We lowered the machine to the ground. Ben flipped on the switch. It whirred, but didn't actually do anything. I poured a little water into the bottom of the machine. Still nothing. I gritted my teeth as I thought.

And then Ben did what all genius inventors do when their devices don't work. He smacked it. The machine rattled and then roared alive. The paint pallet started to rotate. I poured more water into the bottom of the machine as the pallet picked up soap and delivered it to the water and the fan. Soapy foam started to build up and blow out from the bottom.

"We did it!" I yelled as we high-fived. And then we turned back to admire our creation.

We both stared at the machine. "That's not a lot of foam," Ben said, shaking his head.

"Well, there will be more water, but I see your point." I flipped the switch off. "Do you have an old hose?"

Ben thought for a minute. "Yeah, out by the shed. Why?"

"Because I just figured out how to amplify our foam," I said with a smile.

"How?"

"We're gonna have to steal a boatload of soap from Zorch." Gulp.

18

It was Thursday, October 30th, the day before the Halloween dance. It was go time. We still hadn't stolen the barrel of soap from Zorch yet. It was a risk, but we wanted to make sure we didn't get it and then lose it before we needed it. We had to hide it and use it on school grounds.

That morning, Ben and I left for school early. My brother and parents thought we were going to work on a science project. We were, but it wasn't exactly school approved. We rolled the machine from Ben's house to school on top of an old red wagon. We left it in the woods, just off the school grounds. I hoped nobody would mess with it. Getting the machine there was the easy part. We had to set it up during the dance after my brother started to flood the gym, but before any teachers or chaperones shut it down. And we still had to steal the soap from Zorch. That was our afternoon plan.

After school let out, I gathered my things and headed over to Zorch's lair. I knocked on the open door and peeked my head in. "Hello?" I called out. There was no response. I took a few steps in and called out again. I wasn't sure if Zorch wasn't there or just doing something in the back. I wondered if I could just roll the soap right out the back door then and there, easy peasy. I also ran the risk of rolling the soap out the back door right into Zorch. So I decided to stick to the plan.

I questioned whether or not I should open up the back door for Ben and distract Zorch when he came back, but then I heard a deep, muffled voice shout, "Hey!" I froze. "Who said you could be in here?"

I turned around, not sure if I needed to change my underwear or not. Unfortunately, I was not wearing one of my great-aunt Catherine's diapers. I saw a huge grin across Zorch's face. "Gotcha," he said.

I shook my head and smiled. Not because he got me, but because I was pretty certain I hadn't peed in my pants. "Sorry, I thought you might be in the back."

"Nope. What's up?"

"Umm," I stammered. I actually never thought about how I was going to distract Zorch. I only knew that I had to. "I'm a little nervous about the dance tomorrow night. I was hoping you could kinda tell me how it normally works."

"Sure." Zorch walked past me while unzipping his jacket. He took it off and tossed it on a hook. "Have a seat." Zorch plopped into a chair and pointed at the one across from him.

"Thanks," I said as I hesitated. "You know, I'm a little hot. Can I open the back door? Get some air flow in here?"

Zorch waved his hand at me. "Don't bother. I have something much better." He reached behind the chair and flipped the switch on a large fan. "That should do the trick."

"Yeah, okay. Great." Not great. It was a flaming bag of

Derek's poop and I was standing in it. It felt like that, anyway.

I plopped into the chair and looked at Zorch. My brain raced. The whole plan on taking down Derek and having my dance date with Sophie relied on me getting the back door open and I was failing. Miserably.

"So, what do you need to know?" Zorch asked.

"You know, like, umm, what's it like?"

Zorch thought for a moment. "Nothing out of the norm. Boys usually stand on one side of the gym horsing around while the girls are on the other side, twirling their hair, hoping a boy asks them to dance. There's music, juice." He scratched his head. "That's pretty much it."

"Interesting," I said, not sure of what else to say or do. Time was ticking away. And then I had a brilliant idea: Miss Geller's meatloaf. It was the worst. It could turn Superman's stomach of steel into dripping gobs of goo. I stood up and grabbed my stomach. "Ugh, the meatloaf today...I should probably open the back door, if you know what I mean."

Zorch frowned, but said, "Okay."

I hurried around an overstocked wall of shelves and pushed open the door. I kicked the door stop underneath it and peeked around the corner to see Ben waiting. I gave him the thumbs up and headed back to Zorch.

"You alright?" Zorch asked, concerned.

I slipped into my chair and made it seem like I might puke on my shoes. "I don't know what happened. Just came on like a runaway train. I'll be okay."

"Funny, I always love Miss Geller's meatloaf," Zorch said and shrugged. I almost puked just thinking about the meatloaf, let alone eating it.

I didn't know what else to say to Zorch, but I needed to keep him occupied until Ben could get the soap. In the midst of our silence, I heard a clank and some shuffling over by the door.

"What the?" Zorch said and stood up.

I didn't know what to do, so I did the first thing that came to my mind. I fake hurled. Like I was trying to win an Oscar. I bent over at the waist, blocking Zorch's path and yelled, "Hwlaaahh!"

He tried to scoot past me, so I grabbed his leg with my left arm and wrapped it around his leg as I tried to regurgitate something, anything. But nothing. Zorch wiggled his leg. I tried to hold on, but it was getting a little suspicious. If I tried any harder, it would've escalated to an all-out wrestling match, so I let go. Zorch hurdled me and headed to the door.

I wanted to see what was going on, but I couldn't just turn off the fake hurling, so I rushed back to his luxury spigot sticking out of the wall. I looked over at the doorway as I passed by. Ben was gone. And so was the soap. I continued onto the spigot and washed my hands, hoping that Zorch didn't realize the soap was missing. I sensed Zorch walk up behind me. I didn't know if I had been found out or not. I washed my face, trying to keep the act going as long as possible.

"You okay?"

I turned around and breathed out slow. "I'm really sorry about that, but I feel a little better."

"Good."

"What was that noise?"

"Don't know. Didn't see anything. We got a stupid raccoon running around. Don't normally see it during the day, but who knows."

I shrugged. "Raccoons. You never know." I had no idea what that meant, but Zorch seemed to agree. "Well, I should get home just in case this stomach bug returns. Thanks for the info."

Zorch nodded. "No problem." He rubbed his chin. "Hey, listen. I used to be one of those kids that stayed on the opposite side of the gym from the girls. Don't be like me. Ask a girl to dance."

I thought of Sophie. "Thanks! I will."

Zorch patted me on the shoulder. "See you later, kiddo."

"Bye. See you tomorrow. Thanks again."

I felt bad for duping Zorch, but I didn't think he would let the whole thing happen if he knew Derek was going to flood the gym. I headed out of Zorch's lair and circled back around the school.

I met Ben back in the woods. He was waiting for me. I looked around to see a whole bunch of leaves and branches on top of the machine and the soap barrel. It was hidden decently well, at least from far away. It was the best we were gonna get. T-28 hours until my legendary takedown of Derek Davenport, the Butt-Chinned Bandit.

~

I WAS nervous all day on Friday before the dance. I wasn't sure if it was because I wanted my plan to work (to crush Derek) or if it had to do with my dance date with Sophie. It was probably both. I tried to stay out of trouble and kept my head down all day and thankfully, all of my food. Ben and I went through the plan a hundred times, but it didn't help ease my anxiety.

Keeping my plan from Derek was the hardest part of it all. Despite all the planning, I forgot to put my extra masks for Ben and me in my gym locker, so I had to smuggle two out of the house and into the car. Some people stuff it down their pants, front or back, others in their waistbands. Me? I wrapped them around my ankles. Nobody looks at your ankles. And if they did, all they would say is, "Hey, that Austin Davenport kid has fat ankles." It wouldn't be the worst thing somebody has said about me. And I only really cared about what Derek and Principal Buthaire saw and neither of them cared about my ankles.

I entered the gym tentatively, my wolf man mask on to hide my identity. Derek and my mother were still outside. Music blared and a giant disco ball spun in the center of the dance floor, which was basically empty. There were cardboard cutouts of monsters and vampires scattered throughout the gym. I saw Ben and Sammie across the room, but we wanted to keep our distance. I walked under an archway made of balloons and found my way to the drink table. I grabbed a drink and nearly spilled it all over myself as I realized the tiny hole in my mask was not at all adequate enough to drink from. I wondered how I was getting any air.

I put the drink down and paced in a wide circle, eyeing the entrance for Sophie. She was late. Women. But all was forgiven when I saw her arrive. She looked like a princess, stepping through the archway, which was good because that's what she was going for. She wore a long yellow dress with her hair braided and wrapped atop her head. A tiara held it all in place. I started sweating. Well, it might have been the mask, but it's hard to tell. I suddenly wished I hadn't been a scary wolf. We kinda looked like Belle and the Beast.

She walked over to me, her eyes and tiara glittering from the disco ball. I stepped toward her, lifted my mask to the top of my head, and smiled. "Hi," I said, creatively.

"Hi," she said as she smiled.

"Hi," I repeated.

Sophie laughed. "Hi."

Then my brain started working again. "You look beautiful."

"Thank you. You look...scary."

"With the mask on? Or right now, no mask?" I asked, concerned.

"With the mask."

"Ok, good."

I looked out at the near empty dance floor and said, "Do you want to dance?" I wanted to make sure I at least danced with her once before my brother either ruined the whole thing or the foam party went awry.

"Of course," Sophie said.

I held out my hand. She grabbed it and I put my other hand on her hip. We swayed back and forth to the slow music. I had no idea if I was doing it right, but I followed my mother's pointers from our practice sessions. I felt like a penguin waddling across the ice, trying not to fall on my face, but mom gave me a thumbs up as I rotated in her direction. We waddled around in a circle a few more times. Sophie didn't puke or run out of the room crying, so I was moderately comfortable with my skills.

Then out of the corner of my eye, I saw Derek and Jayden slip out of the gym and into the locker room. It was go time, show time, and take down my bro time, all at the same time. I continued dancing with Sophie. My mind raced. The song wasn't over yet, but I kinda had to go. I had assessed the locker room situation the day before. It was going to be easy to flood with all of the showers and faucets, not to mention toilets. If Derek was resourceful at all, it was going to be quick, too. I didn't have much time to get my machine in place before the water made it to the gym floor and the opportunity to best Derek and Principal Buthaire disappeared.

I saw Ben running toward me. I hoped he could think on his feet, because I didn't want to have to fake a stomach ache in order to cut the dance short. She already had a poor opinion of my bladder after I wet my diaper.

And then the idiot spoke, "Hey, man, your stomach hurt, too? We both had the pepperoni pizza today."

I eyed Sophie and then looked back at Ben. "No, I'm fine."

Ben's eyes bulged. "You sure?"

"Yep. Pretty sure, but if you're not feeling well, maybe I should take you to the locker room."

"Yes," he said, shaking his head.

I looked at Sophie and whispered, "Sorry. Sammie is over there if you want to say hi."

"It's okay. Feel better, Ben."

"Thanks," Ben groaned and grabbed his stomach.

I shook my head and followed him closely. "Why did I have to have a stomach ache, too? Why couldn't it been just you?" I whisper shouted at him. He just shrugged.

I steered him around behind my mother without being seen and then we ducked behind a cardboard cutout of some sort of ghoul. I bent down and swapped masks under my left pant leg. We couldn't be too careful. We would be like ghosts, hiding in the shadows, changing masks twice, maybe three times. That was it really, but it was middle school. Kids got confused over A days and B days. Nobody would know who the perpetrators were with different masks. Or at least we hoped.

There was a crowd of boys just outside the locker room pretending that there wasn't a crowd of girls across the gym waiting to be asked to dance. They were the perfect cover. I waited near them while Ben slipped a piece of oak tag behind the vent that led to the locker room. It would allow a large foam build up for party time.

My brother and Jayden slipped out quietly one at a time, looked around, and then headed off into different directions. I tapped Ben on the shoulder and he followed me into the locker room. The sound of water pouring onto the floor echoed throughout the empty, tiled room. Water was starting to cover the floor, but we had enough time to get our mission done, even though we would have to work fast.

"Remember," I whispered, "if we need to pull the plug, pull the fire alarm."

"Dude, I taught *you* that," Ben whispered back.

I jogged across a still dry area of the floor to the exit door on our way to our equipment while Ben placed a towel by the front door to keep all the water in until we were ready to unleash our foam blast. I pushed the door open and held it for Ben. He followed closely behind me out into the night. My heart sank when I heard the door clank shut.

I turned around and stared at Ben. "How are we supposed to get back in?"

"I thought you were holding it."

"I was. For you." I was pretty annoyed and made faces at him under my mask.

We were trapped outside and time was running out.

19

I stood outside the locker room, the cold air whipping across the courtyard. I pulled on the door handle, which of course, didn't open. I looked up above the door line and noticed the windows were open. It was going to be a tight squeeze and high up. The entrance was at least eight feet, thankfully with lockers on the other side, to climb onto.

I stood in front of Ben and realized that even though he was the doofus who messed up, I was going to be the one who had to climb through the window back into the locker room. "Turn around. You're going to have to boost me up."

Ben nodded, turned, and leaned against the wall. He grabbed my foot with both hands and lifted me up. I grabbed the window ledge and climbed up onto Ben's shoulders. He grunted in pain. "Hurry up," he said through his mask.

"I'm trying," I groaned as I stepped on top of his head and shimmied up through the window's opening. I rested half in, half out of the window, suspended across the window sill and gripping the lockers.

"Hurry," Ben said. Easy for him to say.

I climbed the rest of the way through with some grunts, groans, and scrapes, but eventually made it down to the wet floor. I broke my butt cheeks on the landing, but everything else was still in good shape. I hopped up and pushed the door open. Again. And then propped it open with a rock. I said, "Let's go!" and took off running to the woods.

We made it to the foam machine as fast as nerds can and wheeled it into the locker room. Water was starting to pour out the back door. It had to be building up by the front door, perhaps even leaking underneath. The towel was probably soaked and if the water level got much higher, it would start running through the slats in the door.

I set up the machine to send foam through the vent into the gym while Ben got the soap. It would build up in the vent while we set off to shut the power. I pushed it into place with a grunt, nearly slipping on the water and smashing my face. I heard the soap container slosh through the water and then Ben huffing behind me.

"Who knew soap could be so heavy?" Ben asked.

I turned and helped him open the lid. We dropped the hose we had connected to the soap dispenser deep into the container. We wanted a lot of foam. The water was nearing the foam line. Ben flipped on the power switch and it whirred into action.

"Vamanos!" I said, taking off for the back door once again.

We slipped around the back of the gym and entered through the archway once again. I could hear my sneakers squeak as we walked toward Sophie and Sammie, but the music was so loud, I didn't think it would be a problem.

I walked up to Sophie and casually said, "Hey."

"That was a long time," she said.

I panicked. "I uh, had to do #2." Nice job, Mr. Smooth.

"Ooohkay," Sophie said, scratching her head.

"Okay, I'll tell you." And then I told her what my brother was going to do and that we were going to redirect his sinisterness into awesomeness.

"What are you going to do?" she asked, concerned.

"It's a surprise, but I don't want you to think I am ditching you."

"Can I help?"

"I'd rather surprise you...I'll just tell you that it's going to get a little dark in here. Don't move. Stay by the drink table and I'll meet you back there."

"Okay," Sophie said, hesitantly.

"Gotta go. If I'm not back in ten minutes, call my parents. I'll be needing a lawyer."

Sophie's eyes bulged. I turned and speed walked across the gym. My mother eyed me curiously as I walked away from Sophie. I gave her a thumbs up. Thankfully, I had my mask on so she couldn't see the worry on my face.

I headed outside the gym. Kids wandered around, into and out of the gym and the front courtyard. I slowed to a stop in front of Zorch in the hallway and lifted my mask briefly to show him it was me. I hoped he didn't see the sweat on my forehead. I wasn't sure how he was going to feel about all we were about to do or if he would help us. There was a good chance we would have to shut the whole thing down.

"Hey Austin, how's it going? Ask anyone to dance?" Zorch asked.

"Yes. Thanks again for the advice."

"Happy to help."

I looked up at Zorch. "Do you trust me?"

"That depends. Do you know what happened to my soap?" He looked at me with a suspecting eye.

I nodded. "Yes. I borrowed some. It's a long story. I'm sorry about that. I should've just asked for your help...I need your help."

"Okay." Zorch paused and studied my face for a moment before continuing, "What do you need?"

"I need your keys no questions asked."

"For what?"

"That's a question. But I will answer it. For love." And total annihilation of my enemies. "I will have them back to you in five minutes. Ten minutes tops."

Zorch studied my face again without saying a word.

I didn't like the silence. I added, "Just so you know, whatever happens, it is going to be better than if I had done nothing. Okay?"

Zorch answered tentatively, "Okay, but if you get caught, you stole them."

"Deal," I said, grabbing the dangling keys and shoving them into my pocket.

"One more thing. If I wanted to shut the power in the gym, would that be in the main office or your lair?"

Zorch took a deep breath, seemingly in an attempt to regain the color in his face.

"Austin, this is above your trust level."

"Okay, how about you shut the power and I'll use the keys for my other...thing."

Zorch nodded. "I don't know why I'm agreeing to this. Are you sure you know what you're doing?"

"Yes." Maybe.

"When?"

"Five minutes." I smiled my best smile. I tried to make

my teeth ding like a toothpaste commercial, but I'm not sure I got it.

"I'm already regretting this," Zorch said, running his fingers through his hair.

"Thanks! Wish me luck."

"Good luck."

I started running down the hall and yelled back, "Don't need it!" And then I realized I was running in the wrong direction. Oops. I turned around, nearly out of energy, but forced myself to sprint past Zorch in the right direction. I looked up at Zorch. "Still don't need it," I yelled before he could say anything.

20

I continued to hustle down the hallway, my sneakers squeaking all the way. I was way out of bounds at that point, so if security wasn't asleep somewhere, there was a chance I could get caught. I slowed to a stop in front of the main office. I grabbed the keys out of my pocket and tried the first one I got my fingers on. I should've asked for some more help from Zorch. I tried a few more keys. None of them worked. And then I heard footsteps. And whistling. Nobody anywhere close to middle school age whistles while they walk down the hall. It was security on the prowl. I continued jamming keys in the door until one finally found its way in. I quickly turned the knob, slipped into the office, and shut the door as the footsteps squeaked around the corner.

I ducked down behind the door, hoping that my black outfit would camouflage me, despite the windows circling the office. The good news was I did everything I was supposed to do since Zorch was going to cut the power. The bad news was that Ben would be there in a few minutes to set up the music and he could get caught, too.

The footsteps got closer and closer. And then they stopped. The security guard had to be just outside the door. There was nothing I could do. It was almost as bad as when I was trapped in The Butt Crack. At least there wasn't a farting computer within earshot.

And then I heard the security guard yell, "Hey! You can't be here!"

Welcome to the party, Ben! I was determined not to let it be another pity party. I had to save him, but how? What would Derek do? Light a bag of poo, no doubt, but I was fresh out. I try not to make a habit of walking around with bags of poo on the off chance I might need to light it on fire.

I reached into my pant leg and put on a glow-in-the-dark ghost mask. Desperate times call for desperate measures. I stood up and opened the door. I walked out into the hallway to see Ben crawl between the security guard's legs.

I sprinted down the hallway, the security guard lumbering behind me. He was big and bulky, but he had long legs. And my best sport was video games, so it was a tight race. I was only a few feet in front. As I turned a corner, heading back to the gym, he reached out and tried to grab me. His fingers brushed up against my sleeve, but he couldn't get a hold on me. I saw a garbage can up ahead. It was my only chance to get away. As I ran past it, I tossed it down behind me.

I looked over my shoulder as the security guard tried to dodge the garbage can, and stumbled forward. His momentum was too great and he crashed shoulder first into the lockers and then down to the ground. As I turned the next corner, I saw the security guard scramble to his feet. He was a tough one! I had enough room to shake him, but I had to be smart. And then Zorch saved my butt. The lights cut out as if we had planned it. Well, we had, but not for that exact moment.

I let out a little whoop of a cheer and continued on. The outside door was closer than the gym door, so I ducked outside. I nearly knocked over Artie Lungren and Cheryl Van Snoogle-Something. I slipped into a crowd of kids outside and squatted down to swap out my mask. The security guard burst through the doors, his breath fogging the air in front of him. I peered through a few legs and saw the man searching the crowd. I stood up, wolf man again, and walked toward him.

As I approached him, I could barely breathe. I was trying not to breathe heavy after that crazy race, but it was hard. Plus, I wasn't getting a whole lot of air through the tiny mouth and nose holes. The security guard looked down at me and then looked away, still searching for the ghost, who had disappeared, well, like a ghost. I smiled under my mask.

Zorch walked up, looking very guilty. I gave him a high-five, transferring the keys to his hand, and walked back into the gym. Inside, the moonlight lit the room dimly through the windows high above us. I slipped past my mother, not wanting her to tell me to go back outside. Everyone was pretty chill or maybe scared stiff that zombies were about to devour us all. It sounds ridiculous, but it *was* Halloween.

Principal Buthaire yelled, "Nothing to worry about, everyone. We will vacate the gym in an orderly fashion."

The chaperones, including my mom, were ushering kids to the front door.

"Nooooo!" I said in slow motion. There could be no vacating! I broke off into a run and rushed to the locker room vent, hydroplaning across the last few feet of the floor before slamming into the wall. I shook my head and regained my senses, then pulled the oak tag out, and tossed it behind the ghoul. Ginormous and glorious gobs of bubbly foam surged out of the vent. I tiptoed across the water toward the drink table and more important, Sophie. I yelled, "Foam party!" to anyone and everyone. Nobody knew what the heck I was talking about.

And then it started to catch on. Kids started chanting, "Foam par-ty. Foam par-ty. Foam par-ty." Not only was nobody vacating the gym, despite lots of yelling by chaperones and Principal Buthaire, but kids were running in from outside to join the foam party.

I slipped behind Sophie and whispered into her ear. "Care to dance, my lady?"

She turned around with a smile. "To what? There's no music."

I raised my hand in the air and held out three fingers. I counted down with my fingers, "Three, two, one. Now." Nothing happened.

Sophie looked at me, her brow furrowed. I was pretty sure she thought I was an idiot. Unfortunately, I was used to girls thinking that about me. I raised my three fingers again and counted down. "I meant, three, two, one. Now." Aaaand nothing. Sophie shook her head and smiled.

Then the glorious sound of music erupted from the school's loudspeaker. I busted out into the funky chicken. It was my celebratory dance. Sophie joined me as we waded through foam up to our knees. Soon, everybody was doing it. Well, except Principal Buthaire, Derek, and his friends.

Principal Buthaire frantically swatted foam out of his way and yelled, "Mr. Zorch! Get the power back on, immediately!"

Zorch ran over to Buthaire. I heard him say, "Sir, that will put the students in danger. The water and electrical outlets aren't a good mix."

I could see Principal Buthaire's eye start to twitch in the moonlight. I thought he might begin to transform into some sort of Halloween creature. Thankfully, he didn't. Perhaps he already was one. But he did morph into a baby. A giant baby with a mustache, having a temper tantrum. His face was beet red and he muttered gibberish as he pushed his way through kids and foam. Derek wasn't far behind, distraught, thoroughly confused, and flat-out beaten.

And then Ben slipped into the gym and joined us on the dance floor, safe and sound. It was one of the best nights of my life.

21

A fter Principal Buthaire cut the music, we messed around in the foam for a while, but eventually the chaperones ushered us out. I stood outside in the courtyard with Sophie, Ben, Sammie, Luke, Dominique Walton, Luke's date, and Just Charles.

Zorch walked over to me. I stepped toward him and looked up, a sheepish look on my face. "Sorry?"

Zorch smiled. "Love trumps my polished floor. Plus, you used soap, so I can't really complain. I'm just thinking about it as a serious cleaning."

"You didn't get in trouble, did you?"

Zorch shook his head. "Nope. Principal Buthaire thinks your brother cut the power. Doesn't know what to make of the foam."

"It's quite the mystery," I said.

"Sure is," Zorch said through a smile. "Have fun tonight and be safe."

"Thanks," I said. "For everything."

"I knew that's what you meant." Zorch gave a wave to my friends and walked away.

I watched him go for a minute. I remembered how scared I was the first time I heard about him. I shook my head, chuckling. I walked back to my friends. "What's the plan?"

"Let's get out of here," Ben said.

Sophie grabbed my hand. As we walked together, I saw Principal Buthaire whisper-yelling at my brother. "What happened?" He stomped his foot.

My brother shrugged defensively. "I didn't do all that."

"Who did?"

"I don't know."

I looked at Sophie and whispered, "I feel really bad about that." I held in my chuckle as I continued walking toward the sidewalk that led to Cherry Avenue.

"I can tell," she said through a laugh. I guess I didn't hide my enjoyment as well as I thought.

"Let's get some pizza. I don't want this night to end. Do you want to go to Frank's?"

"You had me at 'let's get some pizza'," Sophie said with a smile.

As we walked up the path to Frank's, Sophie stopped and turned to me. She looked into my eyes. "That was so awesome. I can't believe you did all that."

"We make a great team," I said, not really sure what to say.

"We do." She smiled and then continued, "But you're pretty awesome all by yourself. I'm not sure you know that."

"Thank you," I said, feeling my face turn red. I was a little embarrassed, but it did feel pretty good to be me. Not because I had Sophie. I *was* happy to be a part of Saustin, but I was proud to be just Austin, too. I wasn't going to make a big deal about it like Just Charles, but I did like feeling good about me.

And then I felt a whole lot better about me. Sophie leaned in and kissed my cheek. I almost passed out. My brain stopped working for a second. And I have a big brain. But you already knew that. She looked at my frozen face and frowned. "Austin? Are you okay?"

I shook my head and woke up. "I'm fabulous! Never better." I smiled.

Inside, we met up with Ben, Sammie, Just Charles, Luke, and Dominique. We all clinked our soda cups in celebration and chowed down. Halfway into my slice, I looked over to see my brother sitting with Jayden looking dejected. His butt chin was smushed in his hands, as he leaned on the table. He stared off into space as Jayden whispered to him.

I put down my pizza and said, "I'll be right back." I could feel everyone staring at me as I walked over to Derek.

"What's up, bro?" I asked as I slid into the seat across from him, with Jayden in between us.

Derek looked at me and said, "I'm gonna get in so much trouble."

"Why's that?" I pretty much knew the answer, but given all he had done, I wasn't going to make it easy on him.

"You don't know?" His voice perked up.

"I know you flooded the gym," I said.

His face dropped again. "Oh, I thought for a minute you didn't know. Can you at least wait until after my football game on Sunday before you tell them?" He looked at me pleadingly.

I so wanted to get him in the worst trouble in the world, grounded for life. Maybe even get him sent to one of those 'Scared Straight' programs where delinquents go to jail to get yelled at by prisoners, but I also wanted a brother. A real one. Not the kind that was my arch nemesis. I wasn't a superhero, so I didn't need a nemesis.

I looked at Derek and said, "Umm, no."

Derek shot lasers at me with his eyes. "You can't wait? Typical."

"I meant I wasn't going to tell Mom and Dad."

Derek's eyes nearly popped out of their sockets. "Really?" he yelled it so loud nearly half the pizza place looked at us.

"What about Principal Buthaire?" I asked, wondering if I could still be the cool brother while Derek still got in trouble.

"He could get in as much trouble as me. Or more. He asked me to do it."

"Pity," I whispered.

"What?"

"Nothing," I forced a smile, remembering being stuck under the desk in the Butt Crack. "I had no idea. So it seems like you get away with it again."

"I guess," Derek said. "Why are you doing this for me?"

I thought for a moment. "Two reasons. Without all of this, I wouldn't have had this amazing night with Sophie. And I'd like for us not to hate each other so much and be real brothers." I looked away, trying not to tear up.

"You're a pretty cool brother," Derek said. Jayden nodded.

"It's about time you figured that out."

Derek put out his hand to shake. "Friends?" he asked, raising his eyebrows.

I grabbed it and shook it. "Bros," I said.

"Bros," he said, smiling. "I like that."

So, there's your happy ending. Evil was thwarted. The good guy got the girl and found his confidence while reuniting with his long-lost brother. All the bows were tied up real nice. After that, Derek still forgot how cool I was on most days, but things were definitely better between us, which was good because right after the dance, my forever arch nemesis, Randy Warblemacher, moved into town. And that's when the mayhem really started. I'll tell you that one next time.

ALSO BY C.T. WALSH

Got Audio?

Want to listen to Middle School Mayhem?

22

BOOK 2 PREVIEW

MIDDLE SCHOOL MAYHEM: SANTUKKAH!

M ayhem [*mey*-hem] noun: A state of rowdy disorder. Better known as middle school. Well, at least mine: Cherry Avenue. I know it sounds all sweet and cuddly, like you just want to pinch its cheeks and make a bunch of strange baby sounds like a weirdo, but you've got to believe me. It's all a bunch of false marketing designed to trick parents into believing that our middle school is a nurturing sanctuary of educational excellence, when, in fact, it's a swamp of tween drama, body odor, and rancid beef. I should probably tell you the whole story, just to make sure you're convinced.

Austin Davenport here and this is my story, with a few fart jokes sprinkled in (and sometimes blasted). Now, you're certainly entitled to your own opinion, but we're gonna get along a lot better if you just accept that I'm the hero of this story. There's really no other way to interpret it, as far as I'm concerned, but some people have a screw loose or might be mesmerized by the optical illusion created by the depth of my brother Derek's butt chin.

Others may be easily hoodwinked by Randy

Warblemacher's Ken-doll good looks or even blinded by Principal Buthaire's oversized mustache. He says his name all snooty and French, like "Booo-tare," but you can probably imagine that us middle schoolers prefer to call him, "Butt Hair," or more formally, "Principal Butt Hair." I mean, not to his face, because that would just be plain rude.

It was November 2nd, the first day back at school after the Halloween dance. If you haven't heard that story, let me just tell you, it was awesome. For me, anyway. But the aftermath? Not so much. Let's just say that when you create a storm, don't be surprised when it rains. Or floods, which was more apt to the situation I was in. I probably should've thought about that before I battled our prison warden/principal, but sometimes a hero doesn't get to choose his time to rise. Events just unfold and the hero is born. To be honest, I was as surprised as everyone else. I'm not your typical hero. I don't have the family butt chin. Brains, snark, and embarrassing myself in front of girls are my superpowers.

Anyway, Principal Buthaire was on the warpath. My friends and I had thwarted his every move to crush our sweet souls. He was determined to find the perpetrators that stopped his evil plot to flood the Halloween dance and turned it into a foam party and I was prime suspect number one. I'm not a bad kid, mind you. But sometimes you have to fight fire with foam. And a Sharpie. The perpetrators also allegedly drew a mustache on a picture of his wife after breaking into his office, The Butt Crack, as it is affectionately known. It was my best artistic work. Allegedly.

Principal Buthaire stood before our entire Phys Ed class, pacing the immaculately-waxed floor as we sat in the bleachers. Mr. Muscalini stood next to him, teary eyed and squeezing a stress ball, muttering, "No pain, no gain," over and over.

Class was on hold until Principal Buthaire interrogated each and every one of us and that just didn't work for Mr. Muscalini. I didn't mind gym being shut down, but I was a little nervous about getting in trouble. Principal Buthaire was likely going to win the Nobel Prize at the end of the year for giving out detentions. Two months into the year, I was his go-to guy, and he was looking for me again.

Ben Gordon, my best friend, leaned over to me and whispered, "Don't let him break you. Admit nothing." He shrugged. "At least that's what they say in the movies."

I nodded, as Principal Buthaire eyed me with disgust. "Good morning," he said to our class as if it were the worst morning he'd ever experienced. "As you may know, hooligans flooded and nearly destroyed this gym on Friday night at the Halloween dance, not to mention broke into the main office and Mr. Zorch's storage facility. Without the excellent work of Mr. Zorch, this gym could've been damaged beyond repair."

Mr. Muscalini let out a tiny whimper. A few kids snickered, which was quickly met by Principal Buthaire's laser eyes.

"A pity," I whispered to Ben. I'm not too keen on things of an athletical nature.

Principal Buthaire locked his eyes on mine and continued, "The perpetrators will be caught and expelled!"

Eyes widened throughout the bleachers. My heart thumped even though I knew what he didn't. I could expose his plot to take down the dance, possibly costing him his job. But I wasn't willing to risk getting kicked out of school, as much as I hated it, because I knew the alternative. My father threatens my brother, Derek, with military school at least once a week. I feared that would be my fate. And that was a fate I would not survive.

"Admit your participation now and you will only be suspended for a month. If I have to find out on my own, and I *will* find out, I will expel you." There were a solid forty kids in the bleachers, but as far as Principal Buthaire was concerned, I was the only one. He continued, "We already have a lot of pieces that are coming together."

I looked around at my classmates. Even kids who had nothing to do with the whole thing were scared.

"If you have any information that helps my investigation, you will be given get-out-of-detention free passes."

Wow. He was serious and possibly desperate. With all of the detentions that Principal Buthaire gives out, a free pass was worth more than gold, at least to middle school kids who have no use for gold.

"Let's start with you, Mr. Gerard."

Jimmy Gerard, normally a tough athlete, and one that had nothing to do with any of this debacle, looked like he was on his way to his own funeral. His shoulders slumped as he walked toward a table and two folding chairs set off to the side of the gym. Principal Buthaire joined him at the table and began the interrogation.

One by one, Principal Buthaire pulled students aside and questioned them about their whereabouts on the night of the dance and their knowledge of foam machines. Given the collection of meat heads in our class, the list of suspects was going to get narrowed down really quick. I sat in the bleachers, biting my nails and waiting for my turn.

"Hey, Gordo. You're up next," Mr. Muscalini said, pointing to Principal Buthaire and then caught sight of his own bicep. He smiled and admired it like a father seeing his baby for the first time. I was surprised he didn't start kissing it. It wouldn't have been the first time.

Ben stood up and whispered shakily, "Stay strong." I hoped he would take his own advice.

I was the last one left. And that was by design. I'm sure Principal Buthaire wanted me to sweat, not to mention to have as much information about what might have happened so that he could expel me by lunch. Chicken Surprise was on the menu, so I wasn't sure what to hope for.

"Davenport," Mr. Muscalini nodded to me. "You're up next." He frowned. "You know Derek Davenport?"

"Yes. He's my brother." I'd told him that at least twenty times before. Apparently, it just didn't compute. And I didn't really blame him. We were so different.

"You sure?"

"Yep, pretty sure. I've been living with him for almost eleven years." My birthday was a month away. I would turn eleven in December while Derek would turn twelve in January.

I was trying to read Ben's facial expressions, but Mr. Muscalini kept interrupting me. "Are you adopted?"

I shook my head with a huff. "No, Mr. Muscalini. I just stink at sports and I don't have a butt on my chin."

He was a little taken aback. He studied my nondescript chin and nodded. I caught Ben moving out of the corner of my eye. He stood up and eyed me. If he was trying to tell me something, he wasn't doing a very good job.

"Good luck, Davenport," Mr. Muscalini said, still scratching his head.

I walked over and slumped into the chair across from my nemesis. Principal Buthaire narrowed his eyes, as he looked me up and down. "I know it was you," he said, matter-of-factly.

I shook my head. "I had nothing to do with it," I lied. "You might want to talk to my brother, though." I knew he wouldn't because he already had. They were in on the whole thing together. I had heard them plot it while I was hiding under his desk in his office, The Butt Crack. It's a long story. I looked up at Principal Buthaire. "I'm sure this all goes back to him. Can I have my free pass now?"

Principal Buthaire laughed, but more at me than with me, because I wasn't laughing at all. "I spoke to Mr. Gifford. He said there are only a handful of students capable of building a foam machine of that magnitude. And two of them were you and Mr. Gordon."

I shrugged casually, but my pulse was pounding. "Yeah, I'm smart, but that doesn't mean I did any of it. Plus, dumb kids have access to YouTube. And who says it wasn't kids from Bear Creek? They're always messing with us around homecoming time."

He studied me without speaking. I didn't want to show weakness or any hint of guilt. I stared right back at him. "I don't like you, Mr. Davenport."

I didn't know how to respond to that, but I felt like it meant I was winning. I decided to needle him a little. I played dumb. "Sir, shouldn't the video cameras have caught the perpetrator on tape?"

Principal Buthaire looked like he might be sick. "Unfortunately, the system was down due to a software error."

"Too bad," I said, knowing full well that I was the one who erased the software after breaking into his office.

"We are investigating the source of that error as we speak," he said, hopeful.

I didn't like the sound of that, but it appeared as if he had little or no evidence about either incident, so I was likely in the clear. And then thankfully, the bell rang. Class was over. I stood up and looked at Principal Buthaire expectantly. He didn't say anything.

"Sir, I need to get to my next class."

"We're finished when I say we're finished." He stared at me for a moment. "I'm watching you, Mr. Davenport."

Not without your cameras, I thought.

"Sit down," he said, sternly.

I slid back into my chair. I looked over at the rest of my classmates who were rushing toward the exits.

I stared at Principal Buthaire, waiting for him to say something. Anything. "Sir, I'm going to be late."

He acted like he hadn't heard me say anything. He checked his watch, straightened his tie, and tapped his fingers on the table.

Three minutes later, the bell rang. It was the longest three minutes of my life. "You can go now," he said.

"Can I have a late pass?" I asked.

Principal Buthaire smiled. "Oh, you're late." He traced his mustache with his fingers. "Detention!" he yelled at the top of his lungs.

"You forced me to be here!"

He tore off a detention slip from his pad and handed it to me. I bit my tongue, knowing it wasn't a great time to ask if his vendetta against me was worth single handedly destroying the environment. I grabbed the slip, stuffed it into my pocket, and hustled off in a huff.

Principal Buthaire called after me, "Have a lovely day, Mr. Davenport!" His evil cackle echoed throughout the gym.

ABOUT THE AUTHOR

C.T. Walsh is the author of the Middle School Mayhem Series, a total twelve hilarious adventures of Austin Davenport and his friends.

Besides writing fun, snarky humor and the occasionally-frequent fart joke, C.T. loves spending time with his family, coaching his kids' various sports, and successfully turning seemingly unsandwichable things into spectacular sandwiches, while also claiming that he never eats carbs. He assures you, it's not easy to do. C.T. knows what you're thinking: this guy sounds complex, a little bit mysterious, and maybe even dashingly handsome, if you haven't been to the optometrist in a while. And you might be right.

C.T. finds it weird to write about himself in the third person, so he is going to stop doing that now.

You can learn more about C.T. (oops) at ctwalsh.fun

 facebook.com/ctwalshauthor

goodreads.com/ctwalsh

 instagram.com/ctwalshauthor